SEP   2003

LT Fic LORRIMER
Lorrimer, Claire.
The faithful heart /

✓

|| | ||| ||||| | ||||| | ||| | ||| ||||||||||||| || |||
◁ **W9-CSB-901**

THE FAITHFUL HEART

WITHDRAWN

THE FAITHFUL HEART

Claire Lorrimer

Chivers Press   •   Thorndike Press
Bath, England   Waterville, Maine USA

ALAMEDA FREE LIBRARY
2200-A CENTRAL AVENUE
ALAMEDA, CA 94501

This Large Print edition is published by Chivers Press, England, and by Thorndike Press, USA.

Published in 2003 in the U.K. by arrangement with the author.

Published in 2003 in the U.S. by arrangement with Claire Lorrimer.

U.K. Hardcover   ISBN 0–7540–8985–1   (Chivers Large Print)
U.K. Softcover   ISBN 0–7540–8986–X   (Camden Large Print)
U.S. Softcover   ISBN 0–7862–5417–3   (General Series)

Copyright © 1957 by Patricia Robins
Copyright © 2002 by Claire Lorrimer

Originally published in 1957 by Patricia Robins under the title *He Is Mine*.

The moral right of the author has been asserted.

All rights reserved.

Except where actual historical events and characters are being described for the story line of this novel, all situations in this publication are fictitious and any resemblance to living persons is purely coincidental.

The text of this Large Print edition is unabridged.
Other aspects of the book may vary from the original edition.

Set in 16 pt. New Times Roman.

Printed in Great Britain on acid-free paper.

British Library Cataloguing in Publication Data available

ISBN 0–7862–5417–3 (lg. print : sc : alk. paper)

CHAPTER ONE

1946

Harriet edged her way self-consciously through the noisy, laughing groups of people thronging the hallway, the fingers of one hand nervously clutching a plate of ice cream. She was not hungry, but going to the dining-room had relieved her of the necessity of standing on the edge of the dance floor where she knew that she looked, as well as felt, a wall-flower.

Now she found a dim, secluded corner on the wide, thickly carpeted stairway that led up to the gallery where perhaps she would not be seen or noticed for a little while. Above all, she did not wish to be seen by her mother who was somewhere amongst the crowd that had been invited to Jennifer Highbury's coming-out party.

Miserably, Harriet reflected that it would not be long before she would be facing this same kind of ordeal again, only it would be worse because *she* would be the focus of all eyes and it would be *her* coming-out dance. Really, she had not wanted to be here tonight, but since she and Jennifer, although a year older, were best friends, Jennifer had insisted she should come. As for Harriet's mother, Mrs Harold Carruthers, she had jumped at the

1

chance of 'trying out' her daughter, as she termed it.

No one knew better than Harriet what a hopeless failure she was at this sort of thing. Basically honest, she found it almost impossible to pretend. The artificiality of this old-fashioned aspect of society life went so much against the grain that it was little less than torture for her to try to adapt herself to it.

But she did try. For six months she had done her best because more than anything in the world she wanted to please the mother she adored. Even now, while she half-dreaded seeing her, the loving affectionate part of her nature admitted that her mother was the prettiest, most charming woman in the world. If only she could be more like her, Harriet wished for the thousandth time. If only she had that same grace and poise, that genius with clothes, the flair for colour, the unfailing chic! If only she had been a mere five-foot-two instead of five-ten and been born with slim, small hands and feet, a beautiful piquant face! Much as she had loved her father, Harriet had often wished during these last few months after leaving school that she had been less like him physically. He had been a fine-looking man, tall, upright, athletic; Harriet was every inch his daughter. It wouldn't have mattered if she had been a boy. How often Mrs Carruthers said that! But Harriet knew it was not only her physical resemblance to her father that

2

disappointed her mother; it was that she resembled him in character, too.

He had been a reticent man, quiet, a lover of the country and animals, deriving his chief enjoyment from hunting and shooting in the season, from his golf all the year round. Harriet could recall so many occasions in the past when her pretty little mother flew into a towering rage because Daddy turned up late from a hunt—too late for some party or other she had arranged.

Harriet, who used to spend every possible moment of the holidays at her father's side, would flinch and draw closer to him, away from her mother's fury. But Daddy never seemed to lose his temper or to be in any way put out by the constant reproaches rained down on his head. He would apologize quietly to his wife and hurry away as soon as he could to his own rooms, after giving Harriet a smile and comforting pat on the shoulder.

Now, whenever her mother's disapproval was centred on *her*, Harriet would half-consciously try to emulate her father. She would stand quietly, without answering back, and apologize once the storm was over. It seemed as if she had continually apologized ever since she left school six months ago and her mother had started to take a real interest in her, for Harriet seemed fated to do the wrong thing.

First, her clothes . . .

'We must buy you a complete wardrobe, Harriet. It'll be fun. We'll go to London tomorrow and make a start. *Oh*, that ghastly school uniform!'

Thrilled at the thought of her first grown-up outfit, Harriet had set off with her mother eagerly. But somehow it hadn't been fun at all. Everything her mother liked and thought suitable for a young *débutante* seemed to look awful on Harriet's over-tall, over-thin schoolgirlish figure. She, herself, favoured less fussy, more tailored clothes. But Mrs Carruthers, her wishes for once getting the better of her dress-sense, kept insisting on the organdies, the frills, the little-girlie frocks, all of which destroyed what few attractions Harriet possessed.

Harriet's Aunt Ethel, her father's sister, had once told her when Harriet bemoaned her plainness, 'You may not be *pretty*, Harriet dear, but you have other assets worth a deal more. Prettiness does not last, you know, and while it can help a girl find a man, it won't keep him. Remember *that*,' the sensible woman had said.

'But, Aunt Ethel, what's the use of being nice inside you if it doesn't show outside?' the seventeen-year-old girl had asked wretchedly.

'But it does show in you, Harriet. You have the loveliest eyes I've ever seen . . . no, that's not quite true, your father has them. You have his fascinating green eyes. Your hair may be

4

straight, but it is beautiful—the colour of copper-beech. A good cut and perm will make you the envy of every woman you meet. And once you fill out a little and lose that lanky, bony look, you'll have a figure every woman will envy, too.'

'I'm far too tall!' Harriet wailed, repeating her mother's most common complaint.

'No, Harriet! You have the height demanded of model girls. You know, my dear, you mustn't try to emulate your mother. She may be a very pretty woman but her build is *petite*. Yours is not. Just be yourself, dear child. I assure you you won't be sorry in the future.'

But this was the present and Harriet *was* sorry. Being 'herself' did not please her mother as Aunt Ethel imagined it should. No use Harriet protesting that she didn't want a coming-out party . . . that she preferred country life, her horses, her riding, to dances or cocktail parties; no use begging to be allowed to go to her room and read when her mother was entertaining; no use pleading to have a quiet holiday in Brittany rather than a fashionable one in Monte Carlo or Cannes. Mrs Carruthers made it quite plain to Harriet that 'being herself' was no longer desirable.

'You're not a schoolgirl now, Harriet. You must try to be more adult. Burying yourself in the country won't get you a husband you know and, anyway, men don't like *horsey* women!'

'But, Mummy, I don't want a husband!'

Mrs Carruthers gave an angry little snort:

'Nonsense! Every girl wants to make a good match, and my daughter is not going to be left on the shelf. You're seventeen and next autumn you'll be coming out. For goodness' sake try to *fit in* better. You stand around like a gawky schoolgirl with a tortured expression on your face, all fingers and thumbs. I don't wonder Lady Pomfrey asked you at tea yesterday when you'd be leaving school and imagined you still there. And, Harriet do walk with your head up and stomach in. Short steps . . . you come into the drawing-room as if you were striding on to the hockey-field!'

A man's voice interrupted this flow of Harriet's thoughts.

'You seem to have found a nice quiet spot!'

Harriet glanced up quickly, the ready colour flaring guiltily into her cheeks. How she hated blushing! *'A gentle flush is attractive, but you go so red, Harriet!'*

'May I join you?'

Harriet put down her untouched ice cream. She made way for the young man who stood looking down at her. She noticed that his eyes were very blue, that they had humour lurking in them, that his voice was gentle and faintly foreign, and that he had fine features. He must be about twenty, she judged, and she was glad of his company. Now, if her mother passed by, it wouldn't matter. She would be delighted that Harriet had found herself a partner.

6

'May I introduce myself? My name is Paul von Murren. I was invited to this party by Lord Highbury but I have very little acquaintance with his daughter Jennifer, in whose honour the party is given.'

'You're not English then?' Harriet asked, and regretted the remark as soon as she had made it for fear it should have sounded rude. But the young man beside her seemed not to notice anything unusual.

'I am Austrian!' he said. 'At the moment I am living in your country because I am studying to be a doctor. I will be here at least for another four years . . . maybe more if I should not pass all my examinations. May I now know your name?'

'I'm Harriet Carruthers!' she answered, no longer feeling shy. It was nice to meet a medical student. Harriet had always been interested in medicine, and at one time had thought she might like to become a nurse after she left school. Unfortunately, her mother had vetoed the idea at first mention of it.

'A nurse? What nonsense, Harriet! It's a hard life and a most unattractive kind of job. Besides, you'd never meet an eligible man in a hospital. If you must have a job, which is quite unnecessary since your father has left us reasonably well provided for, then choose something a little more chic. Certainly not *nursing!*'

Yet Harriet had always felt deep down

7

inside her that she would have found nursing satisfying, rewarding kind of work. Had the war lasted another year, she had meant to persuade her mother to let her join the Red Cross. But the war had ended during her last term at school and put an end to such hopes. Shyly, she mentioned this one-time ambition to Paul von Murren.

He said: 'But there is still time. You are now only seventeen. You have much time left for your training.'

'Unfortunately my mother would never allow it. I have to come out and do the season and I couldn't do that and my training.'

'Come out? Oh, you mean the *début* . . . presented like Lord Highbury's daughter?'

'I'm afraid I shan't be very much like Jennifer!' Harriet said, smiling ruefully. 'She loves this kind of thing. I'm not much good at it.'

'How do you mean . . . to be good at this? There is some special way in which you must behave?'

'Oh, yes!' said Harriet, her large green eyes serious now and deeply concerned. 'You have to know how to say the right things to the right people, how to dance well and dress well, how . . . well, how to be attractive and interesting.'

Paul von Murren looked down at the girl beside him. He handed her a cigarette, which she smilingly refused, lit one for himself and studied her for a moment. Slowly he nodded, his brows knit in concentrated thought.

'Yes, in Vienna we have had all this . . . before the war, of course. Perhaps in time it will come back again. At the moment, we are all too poor for this kind of life so I myself shall avoid this . . . how do you call it . . . social marriage market?'

Harriet looked up. Now her green eyes were dancing delightedly.

'That's exactly what it is! How lucky you are not to have to endure it!'

'I do not think this is necessary for you. You will find the husband you want without all that!' He half-turned and indicated the reception-room whence came the sound of music, voices, laughter.

'Oh, no!' Harriet retorted quickly, and began to quote her mother. 'I love country life. There aren't so many young men there as in London. And I'd never learn how to behave properly if I didn't do a season. I'm afraid I shan't learn very quickly then, either,' she added, sighing. 'I'm nearly always doing the wrong things at the wrong time. I never know what to say to people.'

'You are talking quite easily to me, and I find all you say of great interest,' said the young Austrian medical student. 'I have had many dances this evening with many young ladies but all they have to tell me is about some other dance they have been to, or what they have enjoyed at the theatre. I find this

9

very dull for I do not go much to parties myself, nor have I time for the theatre, although good opera I enjoy.'

'I like the opera too!' Harriet said, her heart warming to him. 'But we don't go often. Mother prefers a play or the cinema.'

'I enjoy theatres and some films, but I have not the money for such things. I am here only because Lord Highbury insists. He knew my father very well in Vienna before the war. My father is dead now . . . he died in a concentration camp during the war,' Paul said, the light fading from his eyes. 'He was a very wonderful man, my father, a great doctor, too. When the Germans came, they wished him to work for them in their experimental hospitals and of course my father refused. At first they did not kill him because they need his knowledge and they hoped he will relent and agree to work. They put him in a concentration camp. Still my father does not give way. They come to him and promise him much money and power but this means nothing to my father who is a patriot and was very brave. They take away his home and land and still he refuses to work for them.'

'And you?' Harriet asked, enthralled by this story.

'I am still a young boy, but my father guesses at what may become of us if the Germans take our country so he transferred much money to this country just before the

10

war to Lord Highbury, to keep for me and my mother. Father could not send us over here for safety as there was no time, but we left Vienna to live in the mountains with his chauffeur who had a cottage in the Tyrol. My mother, he told us, must call herself the chauffeur's wife and I am his son. This saved our lives for the Germans did not discover where we were. Although they tortured many of our friends to find out, no one but my father knew of our hiding-place and until he died my father remained silent. So it is now I have enough money over here in this country for my studies. Lord Highbury had invested carefully for my father. Otherwise we have nothing. There is our country home . . . it is a very beautiful *Schloss* overlooking a big lake in the Tyrol. But first the Germans took everything we had in Vienna, then the Russians our heirlooms and treasures, our money. We had nothing left in our poor martyred Vienna. So, you see, I must live quietly here where I am learning to become a doctor like my father. When I can, I send a little home to my mother, but alas, it is not often! I would like to visit her more often but I cannot do so. When I am a doctor, though, I will go to live in the Tyrol and try to give my mother back all that she lost.'

For a moment, Harriet remained silent, so deeply impressed was she, not only by this tale of human suffering and endurance, but also by this young man's determination to step into his

11

father's shoes. There was a fire inside Paul von Murren, a fire of ambition that she could see nothing would quench. And she had no doubt, hearing Paul's quiet, determined voice, that he meant to succeed.

Impulsively, she put out a hand and touched one of the long brown hands of her companion who, although a total stranger, had come so close to her in this short time.

'I know you will succeed!' she said softly.

He turned his head and looked down at her, as if seeing her for the first time as an inspiration, a symbol of hope. As his eyes gazed into hers he said:

'Earlier this evening I think that I should not have come here. So much money wasted on such a meaningless party: it was making me a little bitter. You see, in Europe—in Austria —there are many people starving . . . and this . . . but no, forgive me. I have no right and now I am not sorry I came. I have met you and . . .' He broke off, suddenly displaying his youth, unable to break through his natural shyness and express exactly what meeting Harriet meant to him. Hesitantly, he recaptured the hand that a moment earlier had touched his. As he did so, he saw the colour rush back to her cheeks.

'I . . . I don't suppose we'll meet again!' She uttered the first words that came to her mind, filling in the silence. 'You see, this is the kind of place where I shall have to spend most of

12

my time.' She broke off, conscious that she had broken one of her mother's rules for behaviour with young men . . . that one did not suggest that another meeting was desirable. One left the running to them.

But her new friend seemed not to notice her gaffe. He held her hand more tightly.

'Could we not meet somewhere else?' he asked. 'I know I have not much time, or much money, but maybe if you enjoy walking, we could go in the park sometimes? Or to the opera? The ballet? In your country, as in ours, it is possible to make the line and not have to pay too much for seats, is it not?'

'You mean *queue*?' Harriet said, laughing but not unkindly. 'Oh, yes, I'd love that. I love walking and I don't mind queueing at all.'

'Then it is agreed?' Paul von Murren said eagerly. 'You must now give me your telephone number so I may ring you. Your mother will permit?'

'Oh, yes!' Harriet said happily. For this would be her first 'date' . . . the first time any young man had shown any interest in her, and it would prove that she wasn't always a failure at parties. Besides, Paul was very good-looking with his fair curly hair and bright blue eyes; he was tall and broad-shouldered and yet slim. And his lips were fine-cut and sensitive. How could her mother, who was always talking of what she considered *handsome* in a man, fail to find this young Austrian attractive?

'Now I write down the number, then we dance!' Paul said, smiling. Harriet's face fell.

'I'm afraid I don't dance well,' she apologized.

He laughed. 'This I do not believe. We shall see. If you are too bad, then we find more ice cream and come back here.'

How easy everything had become! Harriet thought. Her eyes shone happily as she allowed him to lead her towards the ballroom. All the awkwardness, the sensation of fear, seemed to leave her in Paul's company. It no longer mattered even if she could not dance well . . . he wasn't going to abandon her because of that. So, because she was for the first time completely relaxed, she found suddenly that she could dance, she could follow his easy lead, and actually enjoy it.

He held her lightly; responding to the rhythm of the music Harriet felt her whole body flow towards him on the tide of that music. Her heart sang. Her happy eyes saw no man in the room save him.

'Never again shall I believe you when you say you cannot do this or that,' Paul told her after their third dance together. 'You have much natural grace as well as much charm!' he added in his quaint, courteous foreign way.

He could not altogether guess how important such compliments were to this girl for he knew little about her as yet. He could not know how these last months living at home

14

with a mother who was constantly criticizing her had affected the young girl's self-confidence and all but destroyed it. Now, with a few compliments, he had restored something precious to every woman . . . her self-esteem. Her heart would have warmed towards him because of this alone—even had it not been that she found him so personally attractive.

They danced again, this time a haunting old-fashioned waltz that reminded Paul of his own country; of the gaiety that had once been Vienna's. He, in turn, was undergoing a new emotional experience. So much of his youth had been spoiled by hatred, first for the Germans, then for the Russians, and for what these enemies had done to his father, his mother, his friends. He had learned pity, too, for he had been spared little of the horrors of war; the aftermath, the suffering of the refugees, was something he would never forget as long as he lived. Even had the burning ambition to be a doctor not been born in him, the plan would have been ignited by the sight of the sick, the helpless, the tortured, amongst those innocent victims. As it was, during his childhood he had felt a constant desire to grow up quickly so that he could play his part in bringing back peace and happiness to the loved ones in his own country. Maybe this wish to grow older had made him old before his time. He was, he knew, more mature in mind than any of the young men here tonight. He had been deeply conscious of this difference between himself and the young 'debs' and their escorts. A faint feeling of revulsion against what he saw and heard had brought him to the stairs on which he found Harriet in hiding.

Seeing her there, he had been tempted to move away and seek a more solitary place. But she had not at first noticed him. He had been struck by the atmosphere of complete stillness in her attitude. He could see that she had the identical wish to be alone. As he asked permission to sit beside her, he had not considered her attractions as a young woman. He had long since decided to avoid girls and light-hearted romance, for he had neither the time, the money, nor the inclination for feminine society. He was dedicated to his medical studies. But finally he had spoken to Harriet out of curiosity and a strange feeling of kinship was born. The lonely, forlorn-looking girl had captured his interest where the pretty coquettish debutantes had failed.

Now, as he held Harriet in his arms and looked down into those serious, thoughtful green eyes and noticed the flush on her over-thin face, he felt something catch at his heart . . . something he could not yet name. For Paul it was the beginning of a new and great emotion—a first love that would never leave his heart. He was conscious of a strange bond between them: of a desire to protect her from

16

sorrow and to keep that happy smile in her eyes. He wanted to banish for ever the strange sadness and isolation which the girl had revealed after they first met.

'Happy?' he asked gently, and caught his breath at the gratitude that shone in her eyes.

'I've never enjoyed myself so much in my whole life!' she replied. She forgot that her mother would have deplored such honesty and told her that the way to attract a man was to be more subtle, involve him in a long and difficult apprenticeship of guessing *how* she felt. But the cry came from Harriet's heart and many times in later years. when she was forced to curb that impulsive, loving side of her nature, she was to remember this evening and how wonderful it was to let her heart cry aloud and release some of the bitterness of pent-up fears and griefs.

This was an awakening for him, too. It was not surprising that on this occasion they did not pretend or attempt to play love as a game. Neither desired a change of partner. They danced or sat together for the rest of the evening. Time flew by, where, on other such occasions, Paul would long since have gone back to his cheap shabby room near the hospital and Harriet would have sat alone in the Powder Room longing for the moment when her mother would come to find her and say it was time to leave.

This was seldom until the end of a party, for

17

although Mrs Carruthers was still, strictly speaking, in mourning, she made no pretence to her friends that her husband's death had deeply affected her. In some ways, she had been upset. Harry Carruthers had been a good man and extremely kind to her, giving way to every selfish whim, indulging her whenever he could, providing the luxuries that were so important to her, at whatever cost to himself. Lucy Carruthers did not know it, but most of her husband's weakness where she was concerned was actuated not by love, as she supposed, but by his feeling of guilt because he did *not* love her. He never had done so. He had married her after the end of the First World War and had never told her about the one woman he *had* loved . . . and lost, during the war. She had been an ambulance driver in the front lines in France and their affair had been short, intense and complete for them both. When he learned that Joan had been killed by a direct hit on the ambulance she was driving, he had felt that all love died with her. But three more years in the trenches had worn away most of his bitterness and left him lonely and without much purpose except to be done with the horrors of war.

When he came into Lucy's life, he was a bachelor and with a good income and estates. In fact a most eligible man, as well as a good-looking one with a purposeful, manly face and fine physique and a touch of grey already in his

18

hair. She had set her cap at him and, using all the weapons at her disposal, succeeded in bringing him to the altar. She was in the smart set of the frivolous twenties, a pretty, vivacious, girl, not quite twenty-four. He was not entirely proof against such feminine charms and knew nothing then of the selfish shallow egotist beneath the attractive façade. But even during their honeymoon Harold Carruthers had been haunted by his first and only real love, the dead Joan. Because of it he had felt a profound sense of guilt towards his young pretty wife. He realized, of course, on the first morning of their honeymoon, that his feelings for her had been no more than the hungry passion of a lonely man. Desire quenched, there was little left and he was painfully aware that he ought not to have married Lucy.

He need not have worried for she had no fine feelings and had married him first and foremost because he had money and a few titled relations; because she had been the envy of her girl-friends. But she was incapable of real feelings for anyone but herself. She craved admiration and spoiling and her own way. Harold, however, continued to feel guilty and believed that he was responsible; that it was he who had failed to light a fire in pretty Lucy's heart. From that first day until the day he died, he denied her nothing that money could buy. When Harriet came—so-called after his

19

grandmother, who had been Lady Harriet Millington, a famous beauty of the eighties— his little daughter was destined to be a disappointment to Lucy and the great compensation of *his* life. He had become too introverted to offer demonstrations of affection but there was never any need with Harriet for a display of emotions. From infancy she seemed to sense his love for her, and to respond to it. She became his constant companion. So it was Harriet he regretted leaving when a fatal blood condition aggravated by his war wounds set in, and he knew that he was going to die.

It was Harriet who had felt a light fade out of her young life when that black day came, and she mourned him deeply. Her mother had little patience with Harriet's continued grief and gradually the girl had learned, as her father had done, to conceal her emotions. A beautiful widow now, Lucy Carruthers used the fact of Harriet's leaving school as an excuse to start entertaining again, and accepting invitations. And if Harriet knew that, she made no comment, nor did she let her mother know how disloyal she felt it to be so soon after her father's death. Generously, the young girl tried to make herself believe that her still youthful mother was putting on a cheerful countenance for *her* sake; or at worst, trying to drown her sorrow in her social activities.

When Paul asked Harriet about her parents,

20

she tried to explain her great love for her mother as easily as she explained her love for her father. Yet putting her feelings into words, she knew she had failed to make herself clear for Paul looked puzzled.

'She's so pretty and amusing and attractive!' Harriet kept repeating, her cheeks hot. 'I'm afraid I've always been a disappointment to her. She wanted a boy in any case before I was born . . . She had so much difficulty giving birth to me that the doctors advised her not to have another child. So you see, she never had the son she wanted. I don't think it would have mattered so much to her if I'd been the kind of daughter she wanted. But I've never been pretty, and because I've always been shy, I've never really enjoyed going about with Mother, meeting her friends and living her kind of life. I used to prefer being with my father. So I have to try to make up to poor Mummy in other ways. That's one of the reasons it's so important to me to be a success when I'm presented. I *have* to make what she calls a good marriage. I don't think she could bear it if I stayed on the shelf or married a nobody.'

Her voice was light enough, but the young man at her side stiffened involuntarily. He felt faintly disgusted . . . not by Harriet whose innocence was unmistakable, but by the idea of a young, inexperienced girl being thrust on the marriage market as if she were . . . well, a chattel of her mother's. It was really absurd, mid-Victorian. How different Mrs Carruthers must be from his own adored mother! *Gräfin* Greta von Murren was to Paul the most wonderful woman in the world. Once rich, aristocratic, pampered from birth, she had settled with patience and meekness to a life of labour like her chauffeur's wife—the one she had pretended to be during those war years. She had worked like a peasant without complaint. She had taught Paul so many things. Above all she had taught him *values,* never letting him behave as though he was better than the poor boys with whom he used to go to school in the village.

'You have good breeding, Paul, my son, but this alone will not make of you a good man,' she used to say. 'This you must make of yourself. You have not, alas, your father alive to be an example to you. But the greatness of his memory should help you. Make him your model, for he was a good man—good, kind, honest and all that a human being should be. You will learn after the war is over how brave he was. You, too, must be courageous, for life will not be easy.'

She had hidden her fears from him, the terrible fear that her adored husband would never return to her. When at last the war was over and her last faint hopes were dashed for ever, she had hidden her grief as best she could and started again to work for Paul's good. She refused to allow him to remain in

Austria where he might have found an inferior job, and insisted that he should take his medical training. They contacted Lord Highbury, who kindly arranged for Paul to go over to London University. The *Gräfin* had nothing, nobody, once he was gone. But she was a woman without a grain of selfishness in her.

When they parted, she had held him tightly, for the first time letting him see how greatly his leaving affected her. She said to him then:

'You are now a man, Paul, and life is just beginning for you. You are not yet concerned with love—real love—but it will come to you as it comes to most of us once only in a lifetime. When it does, remember that to love truly means to give as well as take from your loved one. It will be difficult for you, for you will not have money or opportunity for marriage for several years yet. But if you should meet the right girl please tell me, my son, for somehow, poor though we are, we shall manage. I am used to poverty now and it does not worry me. I know you wish to be able to give me back what once I had but I value your happiness far far more than I value my comforts. So remember this and go in peace.'

He could picture her as she was then, speaking to him in her room overlooking the quiet lake. She was still beautiful and slender at fifty, with the blue eyes he had inherited. But her hair was snow-white and the lines on her face had been chiselled by pain and tragedy.

He had thought then that he never would marry. No girl could equal his brave and perfect mother. It was for her sake he was so ambitious and he had vowed to himself he would never look at a girl until he saw his mother living at least in some degree of comfort again.

Now, suddenly, he recalled her farewell words. She had guessed that he was just an ordinary fellow for all his ideals, his noble aspirations, and that he would feel as other men did and fall in love.

As Paul led Harriet out through the french windows on to a balcony overlooking deserted London streets, the air cool and fresh in the early morning, he knew that for the time being his ambitions were forgotten. In this quiet hallowed hour of revelation there was only Harriet, a tall, shy English girl with a heart and a soul and a spirit belying the silly frilly dress, the dying flowers in her brown hair.

He turned her towards him, and he read in her large serious eyes no coquetry, no pretence . . . only the innocent expectancy of a young girl awaiting her first kiss! As his lips touched hers, gently and tenderly, he felt a swift rush of exultation. He realized that this was the first kiss for her, and for himself the kiss that unlocked the door of the whole wide world. He knew in this moment that he was in love.

CHAPTER TWO

1954

'For goodness' sake pull yourself together, Harriet! You must be crazy to think this is the way to bring Tony back. Suppose he walked in now and saw you. You look ghastly with your eyes all swollen and not a shred of make-up on your face. I really don't know what's the matter with you. Here you are twenty-five years old and behaving like a child.'

Yes, it's true! Harriet thought wretchedly. Tony always hated it when she cried, in fact if she showed any emotion, unless it were in bed. The physical side of their marriage was all that concerned him and he firmly believed that any emotional upset could be solved by love-making. Maybe she was being childish, just as her mother had said. Maybe it was *she* who lacked something and not Tony.

She gulped down the tears that were choking in her throat and turned her head on the pillow. How pretty her mother looked in that beautiful mink coat and furry cossack hat! How young! She was in her fifties and yet at this moment Harriet felt that her mother looked years younger than she did. Even the brief two-year marriage to Rex Hatherway with its rather unsavoury ending in a divorce court had not left any mark on the pretty, piquant face. Of course, her mother spent a great deal of her time and money in beauty salons, guarding her youthful appearance as other women guarded their jewels. But then, her looks comprised, in a way, Lucy Carruthers' most valuable jewellery. They had got Rex for her, a near-millionaire, two years after Harry Carruthers died. They had not kept him faithful to her, of course, but even that had suited her for she had dragged him through the divorce court and obtained a vast sum of money from him in alimony. Then her slim, sensual beauty attracted Bernard Maybury, a young man only six years older than Harriet, with whom she was now having a most absorbing love-affair. Bernard was very much in love with her but Lucy Carruthers knew her limitations. She knew that she could not go on looking thirty much longer, not even with the aid of cunning plastic surgery: the 'face-lift' that had already played its part. And she intended to keep Bernie. Marriage was the answer, of course, but here her heart was at war with her mind, for to marry again would mean good-bye to Rex's thousands. Bernard had money, of course, but not much in comparison with Rex and so, for the moment, her plans were not quite settled. The *last* thing she wanted at this stage was to have Harriet on her hands.

Irritably, she studied the girl lying on her big

26

double bed. Only last night Bernie's handsome black head had lain there, little though Harriet knew it! If she'd only bother a bit more about her appearance, she wouldn't be unattractive. In fact, Lucy Carruthers had been agreeably surprised at Harriet's development from a gawky adolescent girl into a tall but lithe and quite elegant young woman. If only her nature had developed as well, the mother thought petulantly. But underneath, Harriet remained the shy, introverted schoolgirl. No wonder Tony had grown bored with her. A young man of Tony Harley's charm and love of amusement was bound to break out once in a while. Why couldn't Harriet see that it was *her* fault? She'd been married to Tony for five years. That ought to have taught her a thing or two about him, and men in general.

Of course, the trouble with Harriet was that she was far too intense, too emotional in a deep, serious way that scared them off. Tony was light-hearted, out for a good time and attractive to women. Lucy had been agreeably surprised when Tony met Harriet at a point-to-point and took a serious interest in her, and then more than agreeably surprised a month later when Tony declared that he wanted to marry her. Part of that was no doubt due to Harriet's 'remoteness'. A good many girls chased Tony. Harriet had been different . . . still shut up in the silly depression which had followed that equally silly and unsuitable affair

27

with the German—as Lucy insisted on calling Harriet's Austrian boy-friend. Well, it took Tony two years to arouse Harriet's interest and break down her resistance. Then they got married and Lucy felt deeply relieved. Typical of Harriet, she suddenly swung round and showered her young husband with a lot of sentimental affection he didn't want. On reflection, her daughter had always been weak, compliant, except on that one occasion with the German student—Paul something or other. When she had forbidden Harriet to go on meeting him, Harriet had actually dared to slip out and meet him secretly. She had been unable to see how unsuitable it all was. Even if he was an Austrian and not a German, and from an aristocratic family, what was the good of a lot of foreign blue blood, plus no money? And surely Harriet should have seen for herself that the boy couldn't marry her until he'd qualified and got going as a doctor in private practice.

It was months before Lucy learned how Harriet was secretly meeting Paul von Murren. When she did, and stormed at the girl, Harriet openly and for the first time in her life rebelled.

'I love him, Mummy, and he loves me. Nothing else matters.'

'Oh, but it does, my dear. You are a minor and I expressly forbid you to see him again.'

'You can't stop me, Mummy!'

'I can . . . and will, Harriet. You are under age. A *minor.* Tomorrow I shall make arrangements for you to go to a good finishing-school in Paris. A year there will do you a world of good and knock some of this sentimental rubbish out of your head.'

'I shall wait for him!' Harriet had said finally, tight-lipped and white-faced. 'We'll write to each other. Nothing can stop that.'

Silly Harriet! Had she not suggested a correspondence, her mother might not have thought of it. As it was, Lucy took good care that the excellent *Madame* Rainault who had charge of the finishing-school, stopped all Paul's letters to Harriet. It was easily done . . . just a word from Lucy about an unsuitable affair with a married man and *Madame* had been only too willing to co-operate. Lucy had followed this up by arranging to see Paul von Murren. Lucy listened blandly to his declaration.

'Harriet loves me and I love her. I will do her no harm, Mrs Carruthers. I will dedicate my life to her. We are both willing to wait to be married until I am qualified. My mother has given us her blessing. I will produce for you my mother's letter.'

'Then she has written prematurely!' Lucy had told the young man and smiled her sweet heartless smile. 'You may think you know my child better than I, her mother, know her. Well, you will discover for yourself that what I say is true. She does not want to wait for you. She has asked me to send her away from you. She wishes to go to Paris. She would not tell you herself because she said she knew you would be hurt and unhappy and she's such a silly, kind-hearted girl that she could not bring herself to upset you in the middle of your important examinations. Be sensible, and consider the matter for yourself. Harriet can and will marry any one of a dozen wealthy young English men who can keep her as she has been brought up to expect. What have you to offer her? For years nothing at all. Then what? A tiny income on which to support you *and* your mother and her. How can you raise a family? And Harriet is fond of children—used to a beautiful home. If you really love her, you will let her go, Paul. I am sorry, but you must make the sacrifice for her.'

He had bowed to the inevitable and gone away. Lucy Carruthers wrote to her daughter:

Paul von Murren called today to ask for your address. It seems he has to go back to Austria because his mother is ill. He said he wanted to tell you that since it will be many years before he can finish his medical training, under the circumstances he does not consider it fair to his mother to continue the association with you. He wants, in other words, to be free to put the Gräfin first . . . a very laudable feeling and

30

one which I think you should respect. I told him I would write and tell you this and he preferred to have me do so. He really regretted that you had taken this first love affair quite so seriously. I admit, Harriet darling, that I rather regret many of the harsh remarks I made about him. He seems a very sensible, nice boy and one who certainly isn't enjoying having to hurt you like this. But he hopes, as I do, that it won't be long before you get over it!

She guessed that Harriet's pride would not permit her to write to Paul after that, but made doubly sure by instructing *Madame* to see that Harriet wrote no letters addressed to Paul and received none. *Madame* was cunning and used to chaperoning young girls of good families. Harriet was only just eighteen, and it went without saying that her mother's wishes must be carried out.

Paul never wrote to Harriet again. And the one tearstained appeal she wrote to him got no further than the post-box in the main hall of the school.

A year later, Harriet had come home, a different, more mature Harriet. She never spoke of Paul. That year of unutterable misery had taught her at least one thing . . . to put on a mask for the world.

Her appearance, at least, had benefited by the French influence. She now wore her

31

clothes with a dignity and chic which delighted her mother, who saw for herself that Harriet had, after all, emerged from the ugly-duckling stage to the graceful swan. Harriet had not got her pretty face or vivacity, but there was a quiet serenity about the girl that suited her, a secret look in the big green eyes that lent her a Mona Lisa mysteriousness.

It was those sad, even tragic, eyes that fascinated Tony Harley, among others, and made him determined to bend her to his will.

Her mother could not know that this quiet façade was only the outward shell; that deep down within, Harriet's heart smarted still from the grief of losing Paul and from a desperate loneliness. She had loved Paul with her whole heart, her whole mind. She had learned to trust him unquestioningly and had never doubted his love for her. She would have waited for him . . . that was the cruellest thing of all to bear. She knew, of course, how deeply he loved his mother; how anxiously he had awaited the day when he could at last go to her with his arms full. That he should want to go to her because she was ill, Harriet understood, even to the point of interrupting his all-important studies. But that he could have let her, his chosen love, go so easily out of his life without lifting a hand to keep her, that stunned her. She had tried to make herself believe that she had just not been as important to him as he was to her. He had other interests, his studies, his ambitions, his love for his mother. She had never been jealous of these things in his life, for he had always told her that they were bound up with her . . . with their future together. But finally she had had to realize that she was not of paramount importance to him. So, as her mother had correctly surmised, pride forbade Harriet pleading with him a second time, nor would it now, a year later, even allow her to enquire at the University if Paul von Murren was back again.

Instead, she tried to comply with her mother's wishes; to enjoy the London season and not regret too sadly their country house which had been sold. She had to learn to feel at home in the large flat her mother had rented in Eaton Square. Most of all, she tried to like her new stepfather, Rex. But that was impossible. How could she look at the fat, wealthy American businessman who had so soon replaced her own adored father and not loathe him? She loathed the way he pawed her pretty mother in public; hated most of all the way he tried, when her mother was out, to paw *her*. Later, she was not in the least surprised to hear that her mother had obtained grounds for divorce.

When Tony Harley started to take her out, she went with him gladly . . . anywhere, so that she could be out of the flat and away from the stepfather she could not bear and whose behaviour disgusted her. So absorbed was she in her own wish to escape from the past and the present that she did not start to consider whether she really liked Tony as a person until they had been going out together for over six months—to cocktail parties, dances, Ascot, Henley, Cowes—all the right places. Anywhere where there was a crowd of young people having fun.

It seemed an utterly meaningless life to Harriet, but she led it as eagerly as the others because for her it meant escape from thoughts of Paul; escape from the fat square hands and small unpleasant eyes of her stepfather; from the obvious unhappiness of her pretty mother, who had made a mistake and was paying for it.

It was only a matter of days after her first meeting with Tony that he tried to make love to her. She put a stop to it before he had done more than kiss her cheek.

'We'd better get it straight from the start, Tony. I'm not interested in necking.'

She spoke only the truth, little knowing how provocative such a remark would be to this tall, good-looking, spoilt young man who thought himself irresistible.

'Dash it all, Harriet, I can't believe you're a *prude*!'

'Perhaps I am,' Harriet retorted calmly. 'Anyhow, in my opinion, love-making should concern two people who are in love. As you don't love me and I don't love you, I'd rather

34

leave petting out of our friendship.'

'Hang it, Harriet, at least you can give a chap a kiss!'

But in the end the cool response of her lips had provoked him still more and he knew that sooner or later he'd have to have this cold intriguing girl, whatever the cost, even if it meant marriage. He tried all his charms on her . . . charms that had so far never failed him with any woman. But on Harriet they seemed useless. Experienced as he was, Tony guessed correctly that Harriet was no prude at heart; that beneath her cool exterior there lurked a fire. Yet he seemed unable to ignite it.

One day, maddened by her continued aloofness, Tony caught Harriet roughly in his arms and kissed her with a fierceness in which all his pent-up desire was seething.

'My God, Harriet, you'd drive any man mad!' he told her. 'Haven't you any feelings? Can't you see I'm crazily in love with you and that I can't go on like this?'

It was the first time he had spoken of love and the first time he had broken through the barrier of her mind and shattered its fragile peace. It was as much this fact as the rough passion of Tony's kiss that made her face facts. Tony was not just a good-time playboy with whom she had been going round for months. He was seriously in love.

She saw him now as though for the first time, recognizing how good he was to look at

35

with his dark brown hair and narrow, hazel eyes, straight nose and wide, full mouth. And he had an excellent job. His uncle was a big man in shipping and Tony would one day come into a fortune. She could see now why so many of the girls found him not only very eligible but attractive. He was young, wealthy, amusing, full of fun. Was he perhaps the right man to help her enjoy life again? Could he fill this terrible gap in her heart . . . the void left by Paul when he went out of her life? Could she find happiness with Tony? Could she ever love him, marry him, live with him as his wife?

As if guessing her thoughts, Tony said quickly:

'Give me a chance, Harriet. You never have done. Let me prove how much you mean to me. Let me get near you. You're so damnably remote!'

All right! Harriet thought. All right. What harm can it do? Perhaps I can make him happy. Perhaps I'll learn to be happy, too. I don't want to go on remembering Paul all my life. I want to be able to love and be loved. I'm lonely . . . and Tony wants me . . .'

So it had begun. And Tony, experienced, sophisticated young man of thirty, knew exactly what he was about when it came to making love. There was no hurried, furtive taking of his pleasure in the back of a car. He drove her back to London and took her to his flat. There, with patience at war with passion,

36

he taught Harriet the first lessons of love. He was not unmoved to discover that he was the first man in her life with whom there had been any intimacy. He was selfish, egotistical, spoilt and immoral, but not really bad, and in so far as he was capable of it, he was in love with Harriet. So he was gentle and tender with her, knowing that to be so would bring him his reward.

Within a few days, Harriet was in love . . . In love with all her senses if not with her mind. She could not at this stage of their relationship dissociate the two, for Tony had now become for her the most wonderful person in the whole world. She mistook his skilful love-making for a deeper understanding. She believed that he could only be so good to her because he truly loved and respected her. She did not know that for Tony, love-making was an art which he could practise with the greatest enjoyment. And Harriet was so utterly responsive, giving him back all he wanted from her. Not yet more: for he was still sufficiently attracted to her to find her affection after their love-making both flattering and charming.

She came to his flat two or three evenings a week but would not, as he had begun to suggest, move in to live with him. When he spoke of it, she became remote and withdrawn again and this time, jokingly, he accused her again of being a prude.

'Tony, don't please say that. I'm not a

prude. It's just that I'd rather not live with you before we get married. Perhaps that's old fashioned. Tony, why can't we be married'?'

If Tony looked a bit taken aback, she did not notice it.

'Well, marriage . . .' he began and stopped suddenly. After all, why not? Harriet suited him better than any other girl he'd ever had an affair with. He admired her, he found her innocence touching and they both liked to ride—and go racing and attend all the point-to-points. They had that much in common. He was thirty and his uncle was always on at him to 'settle down'. Besides, it would mean a certain rather difficult situation in his life would be satisfactorily ended. Harriet didn't know about it, of course, but he'd been having an affair for years with a woman now forty . . . a widow with considerable attractions and income. But she'd become very possessive ever since he'd met Harriet. He had cooled off and now she was pressing him to marry *her*. Absurd to think of marriage with a widow ten years his senior, although he had been quite a bit in love with her at one time. All the same, a clinging woman, getting on in years, could be very tiresome; ringing up, trying to see him. If Irene ever turned up at the house one night when Harriet was there, there was no knowing what Harriet would do.

'We'll fix a date in the very near future,' he said, with a smile, drawing her closer against

38

him and touching her long, slender legs. 'Yes, in the near future. God, Harriet, how devilishly attractive you are! I can't keep away from you.'

'I don't want you to keep away!' Harriet murmured, her mouth against his. 'I love you, Tony!'

'And I love you!' he said.

And not even Paul von Murren's sad ghost was there to warn her that those exchanged vows had a hollow ring.

*   *   *

Six months later . . . almost on the day of her mother's divorce from Rex, Harriet became Tony's wife.

Now, five years later, she was no longer a bride; no longer even a newly wed but a disappointed, unhappy wife herself contemplating divorce.

How could she have come to this appalling crisis in her life? she asked herself for the hundredth time. Was her mother right? Was it her fault that Tony had stopped loving her? Had she asked too much of him? Was it too much to expect of any man to return the kind of love she had given Tony these past five years? Or had he never *really* loved her in the way she understood loving?

'The whole trouble with you, Harriet,' her mother was saying flatly, 'is that you are an extremist. It takes a steamroller to get you started, but once moving, there's no stopping you. You must learn to control yourself if you insist on being so abnormal. I know you feel hurt and injured and deceived by Tony. But his affair is only what one expects of a man. I, for one, see that part of the blame lies with you. You're far too intense for him. Men don't want to be bothered by all these *feelings*. If he's gone off for a couple of nights with a chorus girl, I expect it's because she doesn't ask for anything but a night out and some expensive gift as a souvenir.'

Lucy Carruthers, stupid, worthless woman that she was, prided herself on knowing a deal about the opposite sex. She'd learned a lot from her affair with Bernard. He was another Tony who hated to be forced to tell her repeatedly how much he loved her, how beautiful she was or how necessary to him. He only wanted that sort of thing when he was actually making love to her. Harriet would have to learn that too, learn that to hold a man on too tight a rein was the surest way of losing him; unless he was like Harriet's father and there weren't many men of his calibre. Lucy Carruthers had learned *that*, too.

Harriet sat up and started to make up her face, pondering, as she did so, over her mother's words. She felt hopelessly at a loss to know her own mind.

When she had had that terrible row with

Tony last night and found out about the girl he'd taken away for the weekend she'd been quite certain that it was the end of her marriage. It was such a hideous blow to her trusting, loving heart. There had seemed no alternative but to leave him. The second blow came when she told Tony that she could no longer live with him. Instead of asking her to forgive him, or begging her to stay, he'd flung back at her:

'Well, for God's sake, *go*! I'm sick and tired of your nagging. There's no satisfying you, Harriet. Go back to sweet little sympathetic Mama and see if you like that any better!'

Had she nagged at him? Was her mother right? Was it really for Tony to forgive her for expecting too much of love and marriage? Where had she gone wrong? When had things started to go awry? For the first year, at least, she and Tony had been astonishingly happy. He had seemed to find her all that he had hoped for. He asked only to be with her. His love-making was filled with tender delight in her. And she had banished the ghost of Paul and settled down to a blissful life as Mrs Anthony Harley, living in a charming mews cottage in the Sloane Square area; a tiny little house, almost too small for two long-legged people.

At first she hadn't noticed the gradual change. Once or twice when she had turned to him in their large divan bed to put her arms

41

around him, needing not his passion but his tenderness, he had seemed edgy and muttered:

'Don't, Harriet, I'm tired!' She had been dreadfully hurt. But then, he was tired. Both of them were. They had had so many late nights and Tony drank quite heavily. They still pursued the rounds of social gaiety and Harriet had become convinced that they would be happier together if they lived in the country.

Tony had been adamant in his refusal.

'Good heavens, no! I'd be bored to tears. Growing cabbages certainly isn't my line, Harriet. But we'll get a weekend place if you like!'

The little cottage in the Godalming area was, at first anyway, a new lease of life for them both. Tony, and a crowd of his friends, volunteered to spend weekends slapping on paint and paper. They mowed grass, and picked apples, and were amused by the novelty of the pretty Tudor place. Except for the unending stream of friends, without whom Tony never seemed happy, Harriet was in her element. She was really happy for the first time. Gradually she began to stay in the country on Monday mornings when Tony went back to Town. She would remain to clear up, she said. On a Friday she would drive down earlier than Tony in their M.G. to get things ready for him at the weekend. At first the quietness of being alone with a dog and a kitten had been wonderful. Harriet had not realized until then how terribly noisy and rushed their life in London had become. Then Tony's weekends became less frequent. When he did not join her she realised that she was lonely without him. The cottage lost its first charm. In solitude she began to feel that she was growing apart from her husband. They did not like the same kind of life. If she really lived as she wished, she would spend all her time in 'Henry VIII', as they called their new home. She would only go up to the mews in town occasionally for parties or shopping. But country life for more than forty-eight hours bored Tony and his friends. He liked to have a large audience, noise, bustle, entertainment.

Unable to stand the separation from him, Harriet returned to London and tried to enjoy drinking and the parties as he did. She tried to overcome her fatigue, her growing sense of loneliness. She felt that every day she was drifting a little farther away from Tony. She was frightened by it . . . frightened to probe too deeply into the real reasons. Trying to explain this to Tony, she had met only a lack of comprehension and sympathy.

'What *do* you mean, Harriet? Of course I still love you. How many times do I have to tell you so? I wouldn't have married you if I hadn't been in love with you. I don't see what's worrying you.'

Therein lay the trouble. Tony couldn't see

how empty and meaningless their mode of existence seemed to her. There was no purpose in it, no reality. She wanted a quiet, domestic sort of life, the garden and animals.

'Perhaps if we could start a family, Tony—' she began.

'God in heaven, no!' he broke in. 'That's the *last* thing I want. Do stop worrying so, Harriet. I can't think what's the matter with you these days. You seem so different!'

'Perhaps I'm just tired!' Harriet whispered, near to tears but not daring to give way to them for Tony hated women to cry.

'Then why not go down to Henry VIII for a few days and have a good rest. I'll be all right here with Mrs Wood to do the chores. I expect I'll be out to most meals anyway. Go and have a good long rest.'

She felt her heart sink. She looked at him with an appeal that he disregarded. He was looking through a pile of gramophone records in the lounge. He found one he wanted and put it on—a new dance tune. Somehow his indifference hurt her to the quick.

'Tony . . . *darling*, please come down with me . . . just the two of us . . . please, Tony,' she began huskily. 'We haven't been alone together for such ages.'

He glanced at her. She was wearing a blue bathrobe and her hair tumbled to her neck.

Tony's face softened. At moments like this she could still seem very desirable. A weekend alone with her might be fun after all.

'All right, if it'll make you happy!' he said, shrugging, and began to click his fingers like castanets to the music.

She was restored to happiness. But it was short-lived. Thrilled, glowing, excited, she drove down to Godalming with him and arrived late on the Friday night. Tony found wood and lit a vast log fire. There, after drinks on the large comfortable chintz-covered sofa, with the golden glow of the flames flickering up to the dark oak beams, he made love to her; his own passion aroused anew by the intense desire of this strange girl he had married. He did not stop to consider that the real reason for the desperate quality of her demands was prompted by her fear of losing him, of not holding his love. She wanted so much to be close to him in mind as well as body. She needed to ward off the 'shut-out' feeling that he so often gave her.

As always, their love-making brought them together again. Harriet fell asleep, content in his arms. But in the morning she was faced with the old Tony, restless, bored, slightly irritable and, within an hour or two, suggesting they should telephone a couple of their friends to come down to Witley and join them.

But still Harriet could not bring herself to recognize defeat. She tried to carry on, to give in to Tony's every whim. To please him she left Henry VIII. It was shut up and they lived in

45

London again, chasing the bright lights, the drinks parties and cocktail bars as soon as Tony got back from his work.

Harriet's nerves became more and more strained and, despite her efforts to control her real feelings, she suffered from frequent bouts of depression. As always, any display of emotion from her irritated Tony. If they quarrelled and she reproached him for his indifference he failed to understand her attitude.

'What more do you expect, my dear girl? I come home every night. We go out together. I'm faithful to you. I can't see what more you want from a husband.'

'I want *a friend*, Tony! Someone to talk to. A companion. Can't you see that?'

But he hadn't understood. He personally had no need of close personal relationships with anyone. He really could not see what it was that Harriet expected of him. After four years of married life, he began to lose interest even in her physical attractions. It wasn't that she didn't satisfy his needs but his nature craved novelty, the excitement of fresh amorous adventures.

He began to take out an American blonde chorus girl called Lee French whom he used to know. Occasionally, he phoned Harriet to say he was busy at the office and went back with her to her flat. There was no question of his being in love. He was just taking a pleasure the

46

more enjoyable because it was forbidden. Tony's conscience remained untroubled. What Harriet didn't know certainly wouldn't hurt her, he decided.

It had been quite a shock to him when Harriet found out about Lee; although she believed it was only one weekend he had been with her, even that had been enough to throw her off balance and send her rushing round to her mother's flat. Moodily, Tony rang up a bachelor friend and went out to meet him at the nearest bar to drown his sorrows. His chief regret was that there would be a scene. He could bet when he next saw Harriet there'd be one. And besides—he hated to be put in the wrong. It made him resentful.

But Harriet had only one desperate desire. To discover what *she* had done to drive Tony into the arms of a girl like Lee French.

CHAPTER THREE

It was almost worth it, Harriet thought two weeks later; worth the disillusion and agony of that discovery to be back on such good terms with Tony again. She had followed her mother's advice and gone back to Tony the day after the quarrel. She told him that she was prepared to close her eyes to his infidelity and that she was not going to divorce him after all.

She even lowered her pride sufficiently to admit to partial responsibility. That he should have felt the need for another woman in his life must in part be her fault, she declared with humility.

Surprised and grateful, Tony put himself out to be his most charming. He even went so far as to try to please her by suggesting they reopen the Witley cottage and spend a couple of weeks down there alone.

But much as she wanted this, Harriet had learned her lesson. To Tony's renewed surprise and pleasure, she suggested they make a foursome of it. As her mother had foretold, no one was more responsive than Tony when things were going his way. The older woman had also guessed that Tony would not want to be divorced. He had a reputation to keep up, working as he did in his somewhat old-fashioned uncle's firm, and in spite of everything he respected and was fond of his wife.

On their first night after the row he said:

'Look, darling, I'm fed up with the spare bed. I'm coming back into your room. It's so dashed lonely without you.'

She wanted him back; she was lonely too, but deep within her, something recoiled at the idea of Tony making love to her so soon after he had been making love to that other girl. Her pride as well as her fastidiousness prevented her from exhibiting an easy acquiescence to Tony's demands. So, unconsciously, she struck the right note to bring Tony back to her feet. Denied the right to make love to this new inaccessible Harriet, he fell in love with her again. She once more became the object of his desire.

He set out to woo her all over again, sending her flowers, dancing with her, holding her as close as she allowed, paying her charming compliments, alone and in front of their friends. Harriet used to enjoy long talks with him before going to bed so now he lingered willingly enough, hoping the late hour and their proximity might weaken her resolve to banish him indefinitely as a punishment.

During one of these talks, Harriet reiterated her dearest and most secret wish. She was deceived by this new, gentle, adoring Tony, and risked again asking the question that never lay far beneath the surface of her mind. Hesitantly, fearing his reaction might be as stubborn as last time, knowing she was no less vulnerable, she raised the topic again.

'Tony,' she said, her eyes searching his face, 'you've so often told me I'm too nervy, too emotional. I read an article the other day that said that women like me often change after they have a child. Would you hate the idea very much?'

Tony's instinct was to reply in the affirmative but the 'yes' died in his throat. His mind leapt excitedly at this easy way of getting

49

what he wanted. Harriet would sleep with him again if she could have a baby. Well, it might not be such a bad idea. It would keep her happy and occupied and he'd be free to get around alone a bit more—with less chance of being found out. Of course, Harriet must promise that *he* wasn't going to be embroiled with nappies and prams and a squalling kid, but if she wanted one, well, she could have it.

Later, as he lay beside her, half asleep, he congratulated himself on having made the right decision. Instead of Harriet's usual 'Darling Tony, you do really love me, don't you?' she seemed content, wrapped in a new mysterious happiness. If children really meant so much to Harriet, maybe she'd expect less from him, Tony surmised much relieved.

Ignorant of his thoughts, Harriet lay awake long into the night, blissfully planning the future. It was going to be perfect, now more than it had ever been. This was a new Tony, a husband willing to become a father and settle down at last. She had been wrong to try and make him accept this role as soon as they married. He hadn't been ready then. He was such a boy at heart with his party spirit, his passion for what he called 'a good time'. Older than herself by five years, he nevertheless seemed far less mature than she was in many ways. A child would give him the purpose he lacked, a reason for living other than the pursuit of pleasure, a new unselfish attitude to life.

Suddenly, irrelevantly and quite unbidden, the memory of Paul von Murren returned to Harriet. *He* had had a purpose . . . a driving ambition. *He* had been a man dedicated to an ideal; wanting to make something of life; wanting to make the world a better place not so much for himself but for others. He'd wanted to help those millions of helpless, suffering refugees in Europe. For him there had been so little time to spare for frivolous enjoyment. Yet how precious had been those few brief hours they had spent together at Jennifer Highbury's dance! How deeply she, Harriet, had respected, admired and, yes, *loved* the fair, blue-eyed medical student who had drawn so close to her in her childish griefs! It seemed strange, in retrospect, that she should have married a man like Tony—one so utterly different from her first love.

Disturbed, Harriet put the thought of Paul quickly from her. She had been so young at the time, she reflected, so desperately in love, so terribly hurt. It had never once occurred to her to suspect that her mother had any part in the abrupt ending to her friendship with Paul. She had known how deeply Paul felt about his studies and his mother; that he had put these things before his love for *her* had not really surprised Harriet.

Dear Paul, she thought. I hope you're getting where you want. I hope your mother is all right. I hope life is being kind to you!

51

CHAPTER FOUR

In many ways life had been kind to Paul von Murren. He had finished his studies and become a qualified doctor, a junior partner to one of Vienna's leading gynaecologists, a Professor Ricardstein.

At the time of Harriet's reconciliation with her husband he was actually in London taking an advanced degree in the diseases of women. Professor Ricardstein thought so highly of Paul's potential that he had arranged this course and Lord Highbury was financing the enterprise. Meanwhile life was easier in Austria. The country had regained its independence and Paul was at last able to send money regularly to his mother.

Greta von Murren was Paul's inspiration in all that he did. Still beautiful, the highly intelligent and charming woman lived her solitary life in the half-empty *Schloss* overlooking Lake Piller, content with her memories of the husband she had adored, and her hopes for Paul. No one, she knew, could have had a better son. And he was, at last, beginning to reap his reward for six years' unstinted hard work and self-denial. There was only one cloud in the blue sky of Paul's future . . . his lack of any personal life.

Often when at home he would joke with his

mother and tell her she was his 'best girl' . . . the only woman he needed.

'You set such a high standard, Mutti!' he told her, his blue eyes teasing. 'No girl will ever come up to scratch after you!'

But both knew this was not so. Both knew that Paul had never stopped loving the young English girl he had met as a student.

Sometimes the *Gräfin* almost hated Harriet for having come into Paul's life. Yet because Paul had loved her so well, described her so often with love and respect, she could not really hate the young Harriet. She tried, as Paul did, to excuse her, saying again and again: 'She was very young. It was too much to expect a girl of such tender years to wait, maybe six, seven years or more for my boy to marry her. The young can never wait. They are impatient.' Yet Paul had learned the bitter lesson of patience and abnegation. And he had remained true in heart to Harriet. His mother knew it though now he never spoke of her. Had he forgotten her? Surely, she pondered, he must have found some other girl by now. There were many beautiful *Fräuleins* in Vienna, here in the Tyrol, too; girls who would give much for a future husband like Paul von Murren. It was not just through a mother's rose-coloured spectacles that she saw him. Every time he was home on a visit her friends, neighbours, the tradespeople would all say: 'How handsome your son has grown, *Gräfin*

53

von Murren! So like his father . . . such a fine young man. He will break many hearts!'

But Paul seemed to have no interest in breaking hearts. When the *Gräfin* taxed him about it, he would tell her he was far too busy to be bothered by love affairs.

When he returned to London she guessed without his telling her that he would remember Harriet. The girl was probably married by now. To the *Gräfin*'s knowledge, Paul had made no effort to trace Harriet since they parted. Nevertheless, she felt by instinct that he had secretly hoped through all these years to see her again. She tried to hope with him. For to see Harriet now through the eyes of a man of twenty-eight, he might find himself no longer in love with an ideal. Yet she who knew her Paul, knew his constancy of heart and mind. He was so like his father. He might, poor boy, find himself still in love with the English girl who had slipped so abruptly and coldly out of his life.

Once Paul wrote home and mentioned a young Irish nurse whom he had partnered to a hospital dance. For a moment the *Gräfin* hoped that he might have found a new love, but such hopes were dashed as she read on:

'In some ways, Eileen reminds me of Harriet. She has the same wide green eyes.'

Harriet . . . always Harriet.

Thus it was for Paul. No matter how hard or how long he had tried to put the tall, shy

54

schoolgirl out of his mind, he had never succeeded. He had tried his best to forget her. There had been women in his life—brief, flaming moments of passion that burned quickly to ashes. Unhappy hours with girls in London, in Vienna . . . moments he preferred to forget for he had experienced no real feeling for such women. Such affairs had given him physical release, but left him with his old haunting memory of Harriet.

He liked Eileen, the Irish nurse. He managed to meet her on a different plane . . . that of friendship. He knew that she had become genuinely fond of him, too, and he found her good company. If her likeness to Harriet was painful it was also fascinating to him. The hospital and medical matters formed a common topic of conversation, so he was never bored in her company.

Paul genuinely loved his work . . . the rewarding work of caring mainly for expectant mothers and their unborn children. He loved to see the expression on a mother's face when she looked upon her infant for the first time. He was more than compensated by the look of gratitude when she whispered, 'Thank you, Doctor!' He was deeply devoted to his work among the tiny, new-born infants. He studied hard, as he had always done, and became accepted by his colleagues in this teaching hospital in south-west London as the most efficient and brilliant young man of them all.

He little knew that the work that had served to separate him from Harriet was soon to bring him into contact with her again.

His first meeting with Harriet after all the long years of separation was one afternoon in late summer in his pre-natal clinic. There she sat, waiting for examination among the other young women; the once-flowing fine lines of her slim body already distorted, showing the child within her.

Paul, who was standing by one of the nurses looking at a list, recognized her before she saw him. His heart doubled its tempo. Shocked, startled, delighted, he stared at her incredulously. He felt his hands, usually so cool and steady, tremble.

Harriet, *Harriet!* Her name seemed to throb in his throat, part of his very pulse-beat. Harriet here . . . here in his clinic; a married woman soon to be a mother; married and therefore beyond his reach for always. The painful thought drained the colour from his face. Then Harriet turned her head and saw Paul. As she recognized the tall fair man in his short white coat, the blood rushed to her cheeks. She half rose. Their eyes met and held each other's gaze.

She breathed his name on a note of joy to match his.

'Paul!'

Then he was beside her. She stood looking at him and he at her. He saw a new, changed

Harriet. The young thin schoolgirl had become a woman . . . a very beautiful one, and at the moment, enhanced by pregnancy, for Paul she was sacred as well as lovely. To him the expectant mothers were always at their loveliest, their most feminine, their most worthy of a man's respect and tenderness and care.

That Harriet could actually be here in this clinic was still so much of a shock to him that he found difficulty in speaking to her.

'. . . such a wonderful surprise . . .' he stammered.

She gave him her lovely, warm friendly smile from eyes long remembered—so large and green that he could see now how different they were from Eileen's.

'I wondered if and when we should meet again,' she said, her voice happy, her cheeks pink with pleasure at this unexpected meeting. There was, surprisingly to her, no sensation of bitterness in her heart, only delight in being able to renew their acquaintance. How greatly he had changed! she thought. He had grown from a boy into a man . . . a little more fine-drawn, lips stern yet the old humour in the brilliant blue eyes. The instant she had seen him she had felt the same quick warm reaction that the younger Harriet had experienced.

'After all these years! You're not still studying, Paul? You must surely be a fully fledged doctor now.'

57

'Yes!' he said. 'My private practice is in Vienna but I am here in this hospital for a year of further studies.'

She noticed how little was left now of the old foreign accent. Yet he did not look strictly English. The fair hair still curled in unruly fashion over his forehead; there was a courtesy, a deference in his manner, an ease, not always shown by Englishmen.

'And you, Harriet?' Paul still gave her name that foreign intonation, Hari*ette*. No one else had ever pronounced her name quite like that.

'Me? Oh, I am a staid old married woman!' she said, smiling. 'As you see, soon to become a mother!'

Her joy in her pregnancy rang through the casual announcement and he, who was used to reading women's minds, could tell how delighted she was about this coming child. She seemed contented, happy. He was glad. But in that instant, he realized for the first time how completely he had lost her.

He said: 'I must congratulate you. This is your first baby?'

'Yes,' Harriet told him, and followed him into the doctor's consulting-room. Here a nurse was busy with bowls and instruments. Paul's voice and manner became coolly professional as he chatted to Harriet. She told him that she was feeling well and strong and that she had waited six years for this baby.

All doctor now, he questioned her reasons

for coming to the hospital.

'Oh, my own doctor thought it a good idea to have a specialist check me over,' Harriet said, trying unsuccessfully to hide from Paul the panic into which her doctor's casual remark had flung her. She had only three months to go now before her baby was born; the baby she longed for so passionately. If anything *should* go wrong . . . well, it was unthinkable. Life had been so truly wonderful for her since that night Tony had agreed to allow her to start a family. She had been on the friendliest terms with him since she first told him she had definitely become pregnant. Even her changed appearance had failed to irritate him as she had feared it might do or alter his attitude towards her. For the first time in their married life Tony had become undemanding, generous, even tender towards her. Now she could enjoy the peace of Henry VIII and her garden.

*   *   *

What Harriet did not guess was that Tony, true to form, was taking this opportunity to indulge in a satisfying and agreeable love-affair with a new 'flame', a young girl of nineteen.

Audrey Deering was one of the crowd in their London set, an attractive girl who made no demands on him and seemed to feel as he did that going to bed together could be more fun without the ties of matrimony. In fact, the relationship satisfied Audrey as completely as it did him. If his conscience smote him on occasions, it had the effect of making him more tender and affectionate towards Harriet than he would otherwise have been. Fortunately, she was so lost in her new maternal placidity it never occurred to her to question his excuses when he came home late. She had friends of her own to stay at the cottage in Witley. She took it for granted that Tony would want sometimes to be in London among his men friends, and not continually dance attendance at her side. As for Tony agreeing to have this baby, he could see that he had rather cunningly given himself back his bachelor freedom as a result of which he was good-tempered and grateful to Harriet.

She was never slow to respond to his new gentleness and consideration. She tried not to make too many demands on his time and attention. She had never felt closer to him than now or more content with life in general. That Tony had at last allowed her to have this child seemed proof of his genuine love. His surprisingly altered behaviour towards her all this summer was all the further proof her heart demanded. Sure at long last of his love, she lost the need constantly to plague him for repeated declarations.

She was sincere today when she told Paul

how good life was to her.

'I think we'll get Mr Barrow to look at you!' Paul said, seated now at his desk. 'He's the very best here. If there's anything wrong, he'll soon spot it. Wait here with Sister Agnew, Harriet. I'll go and get hold of Wilfred Barrow. He doesn't usually attend these clinics. You really need an appointment to see him, but I'm sure he'll have a look at you if I ask him.'

When Mr Barrow, whom she liked a great deal, had examined her, her secret anxieties were justified. She *might*, he said, have some difficulty giving birth naturally and might need a Caesarian. It was therefore desirable that she should plan to have the baby here in hospital and not in her own home. She had every confidence in Wilfred Barrow. He was older than Paul—a cheerful, kindly physician. He said that, come what may, he would personally deliver her.

'For a friend of Paul's, I could do no less!' he said when she began to express her thanks. 'You see, I am a friend of Paul von Murren and of his wonderful mother. I have spent several holidays in their home. Now put all worries from you, Mrs Harley. You'll certainly have this baby without too much trouble. I'll see to that. Would you like Paul to show you over our new maternity wing? The private rooms where you will be are charmingly decorated—all the most modern equipment.'

As Harriet walked through the long white

61

corridors with Paul at her side, she said impulsively, 'I'm so happy for you, Paul, that you have realized your ambition. It's good to discover that someone whom one has liked, and believed in, has . . . has done well.' Her voice faltered on a note of some embarrassment.

Paul looked down at her; there was a tinge of bitterness in his eyes. Someone she had believed in? Yet she had not had sufficient faith or patience to wait for this day. Only now, actually walking here beside her, could he bring himself to admit that he had hoped all these years to find her again, unmarried, still needing him.

Angrily, he put such thoughts quickly away from him. Absurd ever to have dreamed that a girl like Harriet Carruthers would have remained unmarried all these years! Since obviously her marriage was a success he had no right to regret losing her. For her sake, he should be pleased. If only he could feel so! he thought with a strange ache in his heart.

Yet, in a way, he did find quite a lot of happiness as he took her round the maternity wing. Her reaction to the rows of new-born infants in their cribs was so much his own when he saw those tiny creatures that he felt close to her. He could guess at her impatience, once she saw the young mothers in the public wards feeding their babies, their faces happy and alight with love and pride.

And soon, Harriet would be here among them with *her* baby. For she refused even to contemplate a private room. Tony wouldn't mind. It would be less expensive in the ward. And Mummy was abroad. She could have her child as she wished—the child that should have been his, Paul suddenly reflected, not another man's. The thought of her husband became suddenly a reality and he felt a quick, jealous antipathy towards the unknown man who had married Harriet. What was he like? Was he kind to her? He must be, since she seemed so happy. Perhaps if he met him, Paul thought, he would even learn to count him as a friend.

'It's so wonderful to see you again, Paul,' Harriet said after they came to an end of the visit to the maternity wing. 'And now that we've actually found each other again, we mustn't lose touch.'

'I expect I shall see you quite often when you come here to have your baby!' he said, and he knew that to do this would mean uncertain happiness for *him*.

'Oh, but before that, Paul,' she said brightly. 'I want you to meet my husband. You'll come and see us, won't you? We have a little cottage in Witley, near Godalming, only an hour by train from London. Couldn't you come next weekend, for instance?'

'I am hoping for a few days' leave!' Paul admitted. 'May I ring you, Harriet, perhaps tomorrow? Then I shall know better if I can be free.'

She scribbled the telephone number on a card and gave it to him. He smiled as he read it. 'Henry VIII—what an original name for a house!'

Harriet wondered if he had something he might prefer to do with his free time. After all, they had not met for years. They were really strangers. They must learn to know each other again. And he and Tony must be friends. Tony disliked threesomes. Was Paul by any chance married? She suddenly remembered that she did not know. When, self-consciously, she asked the question, he laughed and shook his head.

She added: 'If there is anyone you'd care to bring down with you, to make up a four, please do bring her, Paul. I'd be so happy to have any friend of yours to stay, too.'

Eileen, Paul thought. *She'd* enjoy it . . . and, yes, four would be better than three. Eileen was in this hospital in another wing. Probably she would be able to manage a twenty-four-hour leave, if not the whole weekend.

'I do know a very nice girl here . . . one of the younger nurses,' he said. 'If you would really like it, Harriet, I will try to arrange to come and see you with Eileen Mallory this weekend as you suggest. But won't it be an imposition?'

'No, I have two spare beds and a wonderful daily and I adore cooking,' Harriet laughed.

'It sounds perfect,' he said. 'Especially if this golden autumn weather continues.'

Harriet held out her hand. 'Good-bye, and thank you for arranging everything for me, Paul . . . with Mr Barrow, I mean. It was good of you.'

He stood on the steps of the hospital watching her drive away in a taxi. He realized that what he had done for her was but a trifle in a new surge of longing to do everything for her. Far from discovering that his feelings for her had existed only in his imagination all these years, he was now painfully aware that his love for Harriet was still alive, real, as strong as, if not stronger than, it had ever been before. And far more hopeless. Harriet could never be his now . . . never. The sooner he put her out of his mind the better.

Finding her a married woman about to have a child altered nothing of his strange feeling of closeness to her. It was inexplicable. It was just there. There could never be anyone else. Perhaps this reunion had been predestined so that he could be of some use to her as a friend, or doctor.

'Oh, Harriet, Harriet!' he thought wretchedly. 'I shouldn't have let you go out of my life. I shouldn't have agreed with your mother that it was best to leave you alone.'

Yet what else could he have done? He could not have married her then. Penniless, a mere student, he could barely support himself in

65

those days, let alone a wife. Besides, her mother would never have permitted it and Harriet was only a child . . . a minor. Even had these drawbacks not existed, Mrs Carruthers had wanted to stop their affair; she had been only too anxious to help Harriet run away from him.

Now, as always when he thought it over, Paul was bewildered by that sudden change of heart in the girl herself. He told himself again that it must have been because she was so young, so new to love; a young girl could easily be persuaded to change her mind. Yet somehow it seemed unlike the Harriet of his remembering. It was all so long ago now. But on this afternoon at the hospital, Paul von Murren found himself projected back into the past.

As if it had been yesterday, he could recall the last afternoon he and Harriet had spent walking on Hampstead Heath. Hand in hand, they had strolled over a carpet of tawny autumn leaves, blue mists on the tree-tops, the tang of bonfires smoking in the soft air. He remembered the crimson coat she had worn and her long straight brown hair—as bronzed as the autumn leaves. She had spoken of their future.

'We'll come here again, won't we, Paul? When you have qualified and before you take me to Austria. I'd like to come back here . . . to this place. I know autumn is supposed to be

66

a sad time of year but I love it because I've been so happy today with you.'

Tenderly, he had told her that they would come back here often; that there would be many more days, walking like this over the Heath, before that long-awaited time when he qualified and could marry her.

She had clung to his arm. 'Sometimes I think I can't bear the thought of the waiting,' she had said. 'Yet I don't really mind because I know our day will come. I know you won't let it be a moment longer than necessary.'

'You don't seem to have many doubts I will pass my exams!' he had said with a smile, his arm about her shoulders.

'Doubts? Of course not, darling. I *know* you'll pass every exam with honours. I know you're going to be a great doctor. And I shall be so proud of you. Oh, Paul, I love you terribly!'

Yes, she had loved him and trusted in his future, in him.

They had walked for an hour or more, and then sat on one of the wooden benches on the hill, their hands locked, her head on his shoulder, sublimely happy without a thought for Mrs Carruthers, who never dreamed that her daughter had been meeting Paul.

How then, after such a day, could she have changed, he asked himself today, all the old wounds reopening, a change that must have been in mind as well as heart? What could have caused her between that day and the next to feel that she couldn't go on waiting? That she did not love him enough? That the waiting might be for nothing? And to escape from him to Paris leaving her mother to tell him what had happened?

Moodily, Paul strolled back into the hospital and along the corridor towards 'Out-patients'. He had never really understood.

He had almost hated Harriet at first, so great had been his bitterness. In the years that followed, the sharp anguish of betrayal had left him. But the love had remained, and the bewilderment. Now he was adult and she was married. He tried to rationalize the whole thing, to believe that it had all been for the best. But it hurt to know that whereas he had never wanted marriage with another girl, she had, apparently, found it easy to forget him and marry somebody else.

What he did not know was that the young Harriet had been led by her mother to believe him lost to her for always. Pride had forbidden her to try to find him again when she came home from Paris. And when he made no effort to trace her, she had supposed love on his side to be dead. Hurt and disillusioned, hopelessly lonely, she had tried to find happiness in Tony's arms.

She had found passion and disillusion once more. But she believed now that all would be well because of the child. So when she drove away from the clinic she thought happily of her first love and without rancour. She was glad that she had asked him to stay at the cottage with this girl-friend of his, this nurse. If only Tony liked Paul, it should be a happy weekend for them all.

CHAPTER FIVE

That same evening, sitting by the log-fire in the charming sitting-room that was full of pink and bronze chrysanthemums from Harriet's garden, they nearly had an argument, the first for months, over the question of the weekend. Secretly Tony had made other plans, a day on the river with Audrey, and he was extremely reluctant to give up the idea.

Harriet pleaded. 'Tony, please, darling! Paul's a very old friend, and besides, he wants especially to meet you.'

'I wish you'd told me earlier, Harriet!' Tony grumbled for the second time. 'I can't possibly put off at a moment's notice this chap I've said I'd meet.'

'I couldn't tell you sooner,' Harriet said, trying not to nag. 'I've been waiting to hear from Paul if he and Eileen could get away.'

'Eileen? Eileen who? His wife?'

'No, darling! One of the nurses from his hospital. I don't remember her surname but she's a girl-friend of Paul's. She'll probably be the prettiest nurse in the hospital, because Paul's good-looking and he'll have made a fine choice, I bet!'

Harriet had learned a long time ago that for Tony, married or not, a pretty girl to flirt with was an essential for the success of any party.

'A man doesn't want to he stuck with his wife all evening, Harriet. It isn't that he doesn't want *to, exactly, but it makes him look so hen-pecked. It doesn't mean anything'* was Tony's explanation when Harriet had first criticized his all too obvious interest in an attractive girl at the first party after their honeymoon. Since then she had learned not to be jealous or hurt but to accept this as one of the normal modes of behaviour among Tony's friends. Strange how she still thought of them as Tony's, never hers.

'Well, I'll give this chap a ring and see if I can put it off till next weekend,' Tony told her half-heartedly. 'All the same, Harriet, I'm not going to promise. I was down last weekend and I'm here tonight. You said you wouldn't mind if I didn't come down again for a few days. I'd planned a day's shooting with the Beltravers in Bolney, too.'

'I know, Tony, but . . .' She broke off. She couldn't explain to him that while she understood that he liked to get away from the domestic routine and go out with his men-friends, Paul might not understand. He would

70

expect her husband to be here if they had weekend guests. She could not bear Paul to think that all was not well between her and her husband. She persisted: 'Do please try and come down on Saturday. I'd be terribly pleased if you would, darling.'

So gradually had her relationship with Tony drifted on to this plane, Harriet had scarcely realized the insecurity and invidiousness of her present position. It had seemed reasonable, when she first knew that she was having a baby, for Tony to leave her here at the cottage alone. She knew that London life was essential to him, that late nights and a lot of drinks and rushing around were wrong for her, an expectant mother. In any case, she had felt rather sick those first three months; in need of the peace and quiet of Henry VIII. At the same time, she knew Tony well enough not to expect *him* to want to live quietly *à deux* at the cottage. He was far too restless.

So Tony often stayed in their mews house and came down to Witley if and when he felt like it. As Tony's energy exhausted her she was really happier to be alone; not to have him there to worry about. It was bad enough having to cook a snack for herself when hunger overcame reluctance, but to sit watching Tony tuck into a man's-size meal was more often than not too much for her.

So she occupied herself, when she felt better, preparing her baby's clothes in the little

71

room she had turned into the nursery; working, planning, and sensibly taking exercise in her garden.

This might have been a time when she would have enjoyed having her mother with her. But Harriet's mother was far too occupied with getting divorced and remarried and finally with keeping herself young for her new young husband to have much time for Harriet. A flying visit to Witley, and Lucy was back in her London flat or on the Continent with Bernard.

Sometimes Harriet felt lonely and desperately in need of Tony's companionship. But she quelled the need, telling herself that it was selfish of her to try to make Tony 'vegetate', as he called it. At least, when he did come down to Witley, he was good-humoured and attentive to her. There had been so little love in Harriet's life, so much grief and disappointment, she was grateful for love when it was offered. And she did not criticize Tony, although she knew some of her friends and her neighbours did so.

Contentedly, Harriet and her good daily, Mrs Pringle, prepared the tiny spare room for Eileen and placed carefully arranged vases of flowers, the last few autumn roses and the first chrysanthemums, on the chintz-frilled dressing-table. Paul would have to have the divan in the living room for they had only the one spare room.

Tony had bought Harriet a small car. He had his own M.G. in town, so Harriet drove in to Godalming to meet Paul's train on Friday evening. It was the end of a lovely day, a touch of frost in the air; the tantalizing smell of wood-smoke from surrounding gardens. She had left a large log-fire burning in the inglenook fireplace at home, and Mrs Pringle to roast the chicken. Everything was prepared and Harriet felt particularly well, despite the baby's weight and activity.

She waited in the car and almost fell asleep. When she opened her eyes it was to hear Paul's voice greeting her.

'I have to apologize for Eileen,' he said, as he opened the car door. 'At the last moment, one of the other nurses fell ill and Eileen has had to go on night duty. But she will be coming down first thing tomorrow morning. I have been so busy this afternoon I simply did not have time to telephone. I only caught this train by the skin of my teeth.'

Harriet, conscious of warm happiness as she saw the young doctor, guided the car away from the station through Godalming to Witley village.

'Perhaps if we ring Tony and explain, he could bring her down by car,' she said. 'He usually comes down about midday!'

Then, suddenly, she realized that without Eileen or Tony she and Paul would be alone together in the cottage. It would certainly

73

make the neighbours gossip, she thought, with a smile, even though she was a prospective mother.

With his old intuitive understanding of her, Paul said suddenly:

'So we shall be alone? I hope this will not be an embarrassment for you, Harriet. I had no idea your husband wouldn't be down.'

'He quite often has to stay in town. We still have our flat up there,' Harriet explained. 'He's terribly sorry but I wasn't able to let him know till yesterday that you *were* coming and he'd already made an important appointment with a business colleague.'

'He works hard?' Paul asked, to help her.

In the dusk he did not see the flush that rose to her cheeks. She did not really know how hard Tony worked. He seemed to get a lot of time off when he wanted it.

'We're there!' said Harriet, glad to be saved the need to reply. He helped her out of the car, lifted his small suitcase and followed her through a wrought-iron gate into a pretty walled garden flanked by chestnut trees. The cottage was whitewashed, half covered in creepers and late purple clematis. He had never seen a more enchanting sight.

'You'll have to eat enough for two, Paul,' she said as she led him into the brightly lit, fire-warmed living-room. 'I can't eat much at night as I get acute indigestion, and now your friend is not coming, *someone* must eat the

74

chicken!'

'I'll eat Eileen's share. I'm always hungry,' he laughed.

Now he looked round the oak-beamed room, his pleasure and approval clearly written on his face. The curtains and covers—chestnut linen with white flowers—and the beautiful rugs, were in perfect taste.

'It's charming!' he said. 'Just the type of place I would love to own myself. You must be very happy here!'

Harriet saw her home as if she were seeing it again for the first time when she had visualized just how she would furnish it, plan it; it had seemed then like her first real *home*. The mews house was filled with modern stuff—ultra-modern furniture, cocktail cabinet, television, radiogram. It was smart but never homely or comfortable. Her home-making instincts had prompted her to make of this cottage all that she secretly longed for—the doll's house the little girl, Harriet, had never possessed.

But Tony was indifferent to the simple beauty of Henry VIII cottage. He found it inconvenient, too small for the friends he brought down, too draughty, ceilings too low. He kept knocking his head on the low beams. Too far from civilization, too quiet and gloomy, except in midsummer—no decent garage for the M.G.

But this evening Harriet could see her home

75

through Paul's approving eyes. He found her remote cottage welcoming, like the log-fire in the iron basket. The old leather-bound books, looking so right on their shelves against the white walls, the big bowl of roses scarlet and glowing in the golden pool of light from the table-lamp.

'Come and see the rest of it, Paul!' she said.

He followed her upstairs, noticed with his quick eye how delightfully she had prepared the guest-room for Eileen with books, flowers, a glass and carafe of water, everything a guest could want. And he was touched by her thoughtfulness. But he was more touched by the sight of the tiny room that she was preparing for her baby. It had been painted a pale primrose yellow between the criss-cross of the oak beams. The organdie curtains were fresh, the carpet a pale yellow; the frilled crib was waiting. The tiny child-size furniture was the palest blue. The effect was one of freshness and homeliness and showed so well Harriet's loving anticipation of her child's birth.

Pain and pleasure both struck anew at Paul's heart. Pleasure at her happiness; pain at his own loss. This might have been his home, his wife, his coming child. Here, with Harriet, he could have found peace and quiet and the home life he longed for but which, for the most part, his work made so impossible. It seemed to him now that he had never really

76

had a home. The mountain chalet had been a hide-out, the big *Schloss* to which they had returned after the war was falling to pieces, damp and dilapidated, no more than a shadow of the elegant home he recalled from his father's day. Since then, he had lived in rooms either here in this country in London, or in Vienna.

In silence he followed Harriet down the stairs where a glass of sherry awaited him. Later, when he had eaten the dinner Mrs Pringle brought in, Harriet sat by the fire with Paul and questioned him about his mother.

'She has quite recovered, Paul? I often wondered how serious her illness was and if, in fact, she did get well again.'

Sitting back in the deep armchair, his pipe going and his eyes staring at the glowing fire, he said with a frown:

'Ill? My mother? I don't think she has ever had a day's illness in her life, Harriet. What made you think so?'

Harriet leant forward to meet his gaze, her chin cupped in her hands, her eyes puzzled.

'But, Paul, that was why you had to go back to Austria, wasn't it? Why you interrupted your medical training in London?'

He shook his head, brows contracted. 'I still don't understand, Harriet. I only went back to Vienna once a year, in the summer, for my holidays. My mother was never ill during that time. Otherwise I was always in London.'

77

Harriet drew a deep breath. Had Paul lied then, just to excuse himself from having to meet her again? Had his mother's illness been fictitious, in order that he could give her a reason for his change of plans? There was no doubting his sincerity tonight. His eyes looked her squarely in the face.

She bit her lip and pushed a log into place.

'I must have made a mistake!' she said with an indifference she was far from feeling. It was so incredible to look back and believe that Paul had had to *lie* in order to get away from her!

'But one does not make mistakes such as this!' Paul went on, determined now to discover what lay behind Harriet's remarks. 'I don't understand how you ever came to think such a thing.'

'It doesn't really matter now . . . so long as the *Gräfin* is well,' Harriet began hurriedly. 'Let's forget about it, Paul.'

'No, it matters very much to me!' he said. Harriet looked up at him in surprise. He continued, 'You must tell me how you came to imagine any such thing as my mother's illness.'

'But I didn't "imagine" it,' Harriet said, her heart beginning to pound. 'After I'd been sent to Paris my mother wrote to me and told me you'd been to see her; to tell her you had to go back to Vienna because your mother was very ill; that you did not know when you would be able to resume your medical training, as you

78

might have to stay and look after the *Gräfin*, and . . . and that you preferred I should not try to get in touch with you.'

'Good *God*!' The protesting, indignant cry was wrung from Paul. At last he understood. He had had to suffer from his loss of Harriet all these years because of the wicked, scheming lies of her unscrupulous mother. Pretty, heartless, mercenary Lucy Carruthers who had wanted to separate him from her daughter. It was unbearable.

'Paul, what is the matter? Are you ill? Is something wrong?' Harriet looked at him with anxiety. Her face, rosy from the fire, paled suddenly. A feeling of apprehension seized her.

He tried to pull himself together . . . to speak calmly. He stood up and turned towards Harriet.

'You say you were *sent* to Paris, Harriet. You did not go because you wished to . . . to run away from me then?'

'Run away . . . from *you*?' Harriet echoed a little stupidly in her surprise. 'But I was in love with you, Paul. I loved you with my whole heart.' Bitterness crept into her tone. 'I trusted you absolutely, and when my mother told me you thought it best for you as well as for me if we never met again, I thought I'd never get over it. I know she always thought our marriage would be unsuitable but I would have waited, no matter how long, if you'd wanted

79

me to.'

'I should have known!' Paul said, his voice low and angry. 'I should never have believed Mrs Carruthers. She told me that you wanted the break and would not wait years to be married. She had us both nicely fooled, didn't she? If it were not for your mother, I . . .' He broke off, flushed, his eyes furious.

Staggered, speechless, Harriet sat staring up at Paul's face. Her own was white now. She was appalled to learn that her mother could have been so base, so deceitful. Her own mother whom she had adored. And Paul had loved her, Harriet. He had gone out of her life believing it to be her wish. But for her mother, they might . . .

Abruptly, Harriet's thoughts came to a halt and her hand went up to her cheeks as full realization came upon her. *But for that, she might have been married to Paul now. There would have been no Tony in her life.* She dared not give voice to such a thought. It reeked of disloyalty.

'I do not like to speak ill of your mother. Harriet,' Paul's indignant voice continued, 'but I think if she were to come to this room now, I'd want to hurt her—make her suffer as I suffered. It is past understanding. For years I was bitter and miserable, thought my life ruined. Even my work could not console me. But for my beloved mother I should not have wanted to go on living. Young though I was,

80

Harriet, that was how I felt about you.'

'Oh, Paul!' she whispered, aghast. And she was aghast not only for him but for herself. Paul was still alone—unmarried. But she had married and still believed herself in love with her husband. Yet deep down within her lay a deep, crying sense of loss . . . loss for what might have been. How could her mother have done such a thing? How *could* she?

No longer the schoolgirl, innocent and affectionate, Harriet had long since stopped worshipping her smart beautiful mother. The years had brought their disillusion where she was concerned. First, her marriage to that horrible Rex. Then the divorce. And Harriet, the sensitive young girl, had suffered the full force of the newspaper attack, washing all Lucy's dirty linen in public because she would try to extract a bit more money from her wealthy husband. And after that, Harriet had discovered her mother's liaison with Bernard. It seemed simple now to believe that her mother might have stooped to anything to gratify her own selfish desires, even to breaking her daughter's heart and wantonly ruining the life of a decent young man like Paul von Murren.

'I'm so terribly sorry, Paul!' Harriet broke out, her long thin fingers locked together, her face a study in shame and misery.

'And I am sorry, too . . . sorry I did not try to find you,' he said. 'I should have known you better. I always found it difficult to reconcile the *you* I believed you to be, and that girl your mother led me to suppose you were. All through the years, I felt inside me that there must be some explanation. How blind I was never to have guessed the truth! But your mother was very clever—even sympathetic— critical of you for being so fickle at heart.'

'Once . . . once I nearly rang up the University . . . when I first came back from Paris!' Harriet said in an agonized voice. 'I wanted so much to know if you were back, Paul. But because I still loved you I was afraid I might seem lacking in pride. You see, Mummy impressed it on me that you had to stay in Vienna and would not welcome a reopening of our affair.'

Paul's hands clenched at his sides. He felt suddenly hot, stifled in the pretty firelit room. What could he say now without telling Harriet his love was as strong today as it had ever been and that only the fact that she was a married woman prevented him from taking her in his arms this moment? But he could not speak . . . must not ever tell her of that love or he would lose her a second time. If there could be no love between them at least there could be friendship. He would always be on call—one friend on whom she could depend if such occasion should arise.

He put a hand on her shoulder and spoke gently, calmly now.

'We must not talk of this again,' he said. 'It took me many years to recover from the loss of you. But now you are married and expecting a child and it seems to have all worked out for the best. Perhaps your mother was right, for I am still not a moneyed man. I would have had very little to offer you.'

Harriet drew in her breath sharply.

'But, Paul, it isn't what you can give a person that matters in a marriage . . . not the material gifts, I mean. It's what you give each other in *other* ways.'

What other ways? she thought, even as she spoke, suddenly struck by the emptiness of those words that had been wrung from her heart. What else had Tony given her but the little luxuries money could buy? Where was the companionship, the understanding, the sympathy, the 'oneness' that had once existed between herself and Paul, young, inexperienced though they were?

She tried loyally to stamp on this thought. Tony was different from Paul. It was wrong to compare them. Silly, too, to imagine what might have been. The young ecstatic love and passion she and Paul had shared might not have continued on such heights after marriage. There had been a time when she and Tony had seemed close . . . before they were married when he had been so much in love with her and she with him. If it had changed since then into something else, well, no doubt most

83

marriages lost that first harmonious rapture and settled down on a less romantic level.

Suddenly, her thoughts swung back to Paul.

'You aren't married!' she said. 'But there is someone in *your* life now, isn't there? This nurse, Eileen?'

He busied himself relighting his pipe and then sat down once more. Eileen! What did she mean to him? It was her likeness to Harriet which had initially attracted him to her. There was never any question of him marrying her. If he could not marry Harriet, he would never take a wife.

'Eileen is a very sweet girl,' he said briefly. 'But I shan't marry, Harriet. I am dedicated to my work.'

'Yes, I see!' she murmured, and believed him, for she had never forgotten Paul's burning ambition to devote his life to medicine. 'Tell me more about yourself, Paul . . . your work.'

Conversation became easy for him then. Discussion of his career took him back to that early work amongst the refugees in the concentration camp near his home. Breathlessly Harriet listened to him. He had been fired by the determination to help them; to improve conditions in his country; to help make the world a better place for the children of the next generation. That was obvious.

'As a doctor I can *do* something!' he said. 'As a good gynaecologist, I can at least ensure the

84

best start in life for the infants . . . and give the finest care to the mothers who bring them into the world. My work is very rewarding, Harriet, even if at times it seems a speck in the ocean of all that needs to be done. You know, I have a big plan for the future, one which lies very close to my heart. My mother has already agreed, but so far we have lacked the money to start it. We intend to turn our castle—all but one wing where my mother would live—into a convalescent home for mothers and their babies. It is so beautiful there in the mountains by the blue waters of the lake—so tranquil, good for the health and mind. Many of these women and children have never been outside the bomb-torn rubble of the Vienna slums.'

'It's a fine idea!' Harriet said. 'How long will it be before you can raise sufficient funds?'

'One . . . two . . . three years, perhaps!' Paul said regretfully. 'Many of the old families like ours in Austria are almost penniless. It is a question of necessities before luxuries. But I am trying myself to raise money for there is so much of it wasted . . . wealthy people in Vienna who suffered little in the war. They come to *Herr* Ricardstein for treatment they really do not need and I step in and put my cause to them. Quite often they give me handsome cheques. It would surprise you, Harriet, what kind of women do exist in this world of ours. They come, the rich society ladies, from all over the world, because

85

Herr Ricardstein is our greatest gynaecologist. Queens and princesses come to him—and such is his skill, his patience, few remain childless. He gives new hope to such poor ladies.'

'He must be a very wonderful man!' Harriet said.

Paul stood up, glancing at his watch.

'Harriet, it is nearly midnight. We have been talking for hours and it is high time you had some sleep. I am quite sure Wilfred Barrow would haul me over the coals if he knew I'd kept you up so late.'

'Why, I've all but forgotten my condition!' Harriet said, laughing. 'I suppose I *am* tired, but time has gone so quickly. It always did in the old days when we started talking. Do you remember?'

Yes! thought Paul. Every moment I ever spent with you flew on silver wings . . . just as time without you has dragged on leaden feet. Oh, Harriet . . . dear, sweet, gentle Harriet, my unhappy schoolgirl grown to radiant womanhood—I love you still so much.

He lifted her hand and kissed it in Continental fashion.

She gave him her wide lovely smile.

'Goodnight, Paul. And . . . I'd like you to know how very happy I am that we should have found each other again after so long. It's wonderful to have your friendship. There are so few people in this world one really seems to want for one's friends. I do hope you'll come down often.'

Lying in the dark, tortured by his thoughts, Paul wondered if he could endure repeated visits to Harriet's home. For he loved her still . . . loved her more, perhaps, than he had done as a mere boy, and one who had had no yardstick by which to gauge her. How could he endure friendship, cool, casual, without love? Better perhaps to break away for the second time. Yet, if his friendship was of any value to her—and she had said that it was so—he was powerless to go.

He hated the woman who had separated them. Harriet's mother she might be but Paul could never forgive Lucy Carruthers . . . never as long as he lived. The young girl of seventeen, his Harriet, had loved him. She had gone on loving him until she met this man, Tony! Paul wrestled with his secret misery and regret. If only he had insisted on seeing her once again . . . forced the real truth from her . . . if . . . if . . . !

He twisted on the divan bed in the fire-warmed sitting room, tortured by the hopelessness of his resuscitated love; by the bitterness of his regrets. He tried to force himself to accept the fact of this marriage. But not knowing more than her husband's name, he could not feel any personal emotion towards the man she had married. Anthony Harley must be a decent fellow that Harriet should love him, Paul ruminated. Yet the very idea of Harriet's intimate life with her husband smote even more cruelly at Paul's heart. He put on the lamp, sat up and smoked, tormented by his thoughts. He reminded himself that Harriet was bearing Harley's child. But when at last he slept, it was to dream that he and Harriet were walking hand in hand by the shining lake in his beloved Tyrol—that as he gently took her arm, she looked up at him with those luminous green eyes, the eyes not of the young girl, but of the woman facing the ordeal of child-birth. 'Oh, Paul,' she said, 'I do hope our baby will be a boy, don't you? I want a son who will be just like you!'

He kissed her forehead, deliriously happy. Then a mist clouded the lake and the dream changed. It was his mother speaking and he, himself, was the infant lying in a pale yellow organdie cot. But his mother's face changed yet again and became Harriet's. It was Harriet's voice filled with tenderness speaking to him. 'It's time to wake up, Paul, wake up ... it's such a beautiful day!'

The dream had become reality. Opening his eyes he saw his hostess standing there at his bedside, a cup of tea in her hand, her face smiling happily. Harriet, so much Mrs Tony Harley, wearing a grey tweed skirt and a white and yellow smock, her brown hair tied back in a ponytail.

'Do you know it's nearly nine-thirty, Paul? My Mrs Pringle will be here any moment.

You'll have to get up and let her do the room. Anyway, it's the most beautiful morning. The sun is shining and the weather forecast is good. After breakfast, we'll go for a walk! I'll take you up on the Hog's Back if you like. I can still walk quite a way and it's good for me, isn't it?'

Nostalgia hit Paul when he found himself up there on the hills, slowly walking beside Harriet. Her bronzed hair blew about her face, her cheeks were rosy from the crisp coolness of the breeze and the sunlight danced in those fabulous eyes. She looked seventeen again, he thought, not a woman about to bring a child into the world. The past caught up with the present. They were back on Hampstead Heath, hand in hand, young, happy, in love with nature and in love with each other. They were filled with the sheer joy of being alive on such a morning . . . with a mutual joy of true companionship, unspoken understanding.

Harriet did not try to fathom the reason for her own soaring spirits. She only knew that she was happy; that she felt particularly well; that it was lovely to be walking like this with Paul again. There was a wonderful feeling of excitement in the air, the freshness, newness and beauty of spring, rather than autumn. It seemed to echo in her heart, not quite as it did in Paul's because he was conscious of his old love for her, but she thought of the coming of her child. Tony was far from her mind. Yet, just now, she did not associate her deep feelings with her old emotional need of Paul. It was a love she had never forgotten but which she never, since she married Tony, imagined might return. She knew only that she was happier this morning than she had been for months. She was content not to try to analyse that happiness. Life had taught her to be a little cynical—not to count on such happiness lasting, but to take it when it came and be grateful to fate.

So Paul walked beside her, trying to forget that this was the woman he loved and would continue to love until he died.

CHAPTER SIX

'Let's all go round to the pub for a drink!' Tony said brightly, bored with the medical trend the conversation had taken since tea. Knowing nothing about doctors or hospitals, he could not join in, and he felt out of the picture. Eileen Mallory and Harriet were both hanging on to Paul's words as if they were important, Tony thought sulkily. He didn't dislike the chap, but he didn't altogether like him, either. He was far too serious to suit Tony's light, frivolous nature. Idealists bored Tony stiff, and the Austrian doctor was obviously such a one.

However, Tony liked the Irish nurse.

Driving down from London with her, he had come to the conclusion that this wasn't going to be such a boring weekend after all. Eileen had true Irish beauty and she was amusing. She laughed at his jokes and made no protest when he drove the M.G. a little faster than he should just to see how she'd take it. Yes, he liked Miss Mallory, and found her laughter and the greenish eyes (like Harriet's, but with more sparkle) provocative. He and she might have quite a bit of fun together given a chance, he decided.

But by six o'clock Tony was in a bad mood. So far, there hadn't been a chance for him to enjoy a flirtation with Eileen. After lunch, Harriet had gone up to rest. But when Tony suggested a walk down towards Enton and that lovely lake there, Paul had taken it for granted the invitation included him. They'd gone as a 'threesome'; a damned bore in Tony's estimation. Now he was trying to get to the Rose and Crown for a round of drinks to cheer the party up.

'But, darling, dinner's nearly ready!' Harriet said. 'Couldn't you all have a gin here?'

'We *could*!' Tony said ungraciously. 'But I thought our guests might find the pub more amusing. Matter of fact, it's a lovely old place . . . well worth seeing.'

'Well, I could delay dinner for half an hour. I can ask Mrs P. to stay a bit longer,' Harriet said, wanting to please him as always. He could be so irritable if he couldn't get his own way.

'Couldn't we see the Rose and Crown tomorrow?' Paul suggested, guessing that Harriet might not feel like helping with the meal later on. She got tired at night, naturally. Her husband should be tactful and see that.

'Never much fun on Sunday morning,' Tony said untruthfully. 'Look, if you don't want to turn out again, you stay and have a gin here with Harriet. I'll run Eileen up for a look-see and a quick one. What about it, Eileen?'

The young nurse hesitated. She had not worked among medical students for four years without learning something about men; men of Tony's type. She had summed him up fairly accurately on that drive down alone with him and she didn't much like what she had discovered. It was all very well for the unmarried ones. It could be fun to have a light-hearted flirtation with them. But Tony was married . . . and to a woman Eileen had liked from their first meeting. Moreover, she had had a brief account from Paul of how *he* had come to know her. He had said nothing of the way he felt about her now, but Eileen knew Paul well enough to come to the conclusion that he was still in love with Harriet. The very tone of voice when he spoke about Harriet gave him away to Eileen who was a perceptive person. So by now Eileen realized reluctantly that her own chances with Paul were not so good as she had once hoped.

She'd hoped for so long that Paul might fall in love with her. Their friendship had developed slowly but steadily. Then one evening, a month or so ago, Paul had told her about Harriet.

'I've never been in love with any girl since!' he had said. 'I don't suppose I will be!'

She had laughed gently.

'I expect you will, Paul. You'll fall "all of a heap" one of these days and won't know what's hit you.'

He had taken her in his arms and kissed her, not as she had hoped he might on the lips, but on both cheeks.

'Perhaps I'll wake up one day and find myself in love with you, Eileen! Your eyes are so very like hers.'

'I suppose that's why you find me attractive!' Eileen had laughed a trifle ruefully. But she had begun to hope. And now, Paul had met his Harriet again.

Eileen wanted to hate Harriet Harley but she found she could not do so. There was too much to admire in the older girl. Eileen could even feel flattered that Paul should ever have thought her like Harriet, since to her, anyway, Harriet Harley seemed lovely. Too tall, perhaps. And, feature by feature, she was not beautiful in the classic sense, but the impression she gave was one of dignity, a serenity of mind; and withal, a depth and sincerity of character.

But as for Tony Harley . . . Eileen's views of him were less favourable. Handsome yes, but too well aware of his own good looks. His mouth gave him away . . . full, sensuous, selfish, a man with money and who indulged himself without much restraint with no time for consideration of others—even of his wife. It was clear enough to Eileen that Tony liked his own way and was used to getting it; clear, too, that Harriet was his slave. During the afternoon, it had been Paul, not Tony, who had put a cushion behind Harriet's back; Paul who had suggested Eileen got the tea while Harriet put her feet up. Tony made few concessions to his wife's condition, and even now he was unconcerned as to whether she wished to delay the dinner and be dragged out on a pub-crawl, or not.

Reluctantly, Eileen stood up and agreed to accompany Tony. She didn't in the least want to go, but she was sufficiently astute to guess Tony's reactions if he was thwarted. She had met his type before. She had little time for such men but she acted now from unselfish motives, knowing that Paul had been looking forward to this weekend and that Harriet would want things to go smoothly.

'Okay—I'll paint the pub red with my host,' she said lightly.

'Is your husband always so energetic?' Paul asked after the two had gone. He substituted the kinder word for *restless*.

Harriet studied her nails.

'Well, yes, I suppose he is. He hates sitting still.'

'Does he read much?' Paul asked, remembering Harriet's penchant for good books and classical music.

'Practically never. He likes an *Esquire* and a dance record,' Harriet laughed without malice. 'He's keen on sport, you know, Paul. He's exceptionally good at games. He likes to play squash in the evenings up in London. He adores ski-ing in the winter. And he loves tennis and sailing in the summer.'

Paul had nothing against a 'sporting' man for he was good at most games himself, and enjoyed being out of doors whenever it was possible. All the same, he decided that Harriet's husband was beginning to show up in a poor light.

Paul had been determined to like Tony for Harriet's sake or at least not to *dislike* him. But the more he saw of the spoiled young man, the less he could understand why Harriet had married him. At first introduction, he had admitted to Tony's good looks and apparent charm, and could see that she might well have fallen in love with him. But those outward appearances belied the real man. The charm fell off when Tony was not doing what he wanted . . . and on closer scrutiny the professional doctor's eyes noted the

95

unmistakable signs of dissipation. Tony looked ten years older than Paul himself, but in fact there was only three years between the two men.

Yet Harriet seemed to adore him. She had been clearly thrilled to greet him when he arrived, fussing round him rather like a mother might fuss over a child home from school, Paul thought. Was he tired after his drive? Would he like a drink before lunch or a meal right away? She had even laid out a pair of slacks, sports shirt and a yellow pullover ready for him to change into. And her only reward had been a casual 'Thanks, darling!' . . . a peck on the cheek for welcome. Then off he had gone to get out his electric portable gramophone and try out a new Rock 'n' Roll record which amused him. He grinned while the noise drowned the voices in the cottage.

At lunch, he had addressed most of his remarks to Eileen, who was looking charming in pale blue tweeds. Her hair curled naturally and was very fair. There were provocative golden freckles sprinkling her short nose. She was ready to laugh at his jokes, which pleased him. But Harriet sat silent, or else busied herself serving the meal. When Paul offered to carry out some dishes, Tony had stopped him and said with his lazy drawl:

'No, sit down, old boy, let her do it . . . she likes it. We could easily afford a living-in cook housekeeper but Harriet prefers to be alone.'

96

'Yes, really, Paul, I like to do this myself!' Harriet cut in with what Paul thought a painful eagerness to agree. He wondered if she might have thought so before her pregnancy, but now she was bound to tire more quickly.

'Well, I'd like to help my hostess!' Paul said firmly, and seized a tray. He was rewarded by a grateful smile from Harriet, who had to admit she was feeling far more lethargic this weekend.

*   *   *

While Tony and Eileen were at the Rose and Crown, Harriet discussed the young nurse.

'She's *nice*, Paul. Are you . . . would it be tactless of me to ask if there's anything serious between you?'

The swift denial that rose to his lips was checked before he spoke. He did not want Harriet to know how deeply he still felt about *her*. Should she do so, she might well refuse to see him again—that had become his secret dread. Let her imagine a romance between himself and Eileen, it would put her at her ease.

'Perhaps!' he said lightly. 'Nothing definite, you know.'

Harriet leaned a tired back against the cushions and sighed.

'She'd be lucky to have you for a husband, Paul. You're obviously domesticated at heart . . . and so good and kind. And she's a

97

darling—a genuine sort of person. I like her very much, Paul.'

'She's a wonderful nurse!' Paul said, looking away from Harriet. 'One of the best in our hospital. Remember you once thought you might enjoy nursing, Harriet?'

'Yes!' She gave a rueful laugh. 'And I *really would* have liked it, Paul. I knew then, young though I was, that it wouldn't be an easy life but I don't think I'd have minded hard work. Still . . . I suppose that is one childish ambition that will never be realized now.'

'To be a mother is just as rewarding a career in itself!' Paul said. 'It'll keep you busy and happy, my dear.'

At the thought of her coming child, her face softened. Watching her, the man thought how much his Harriet had really changed. The thin, troubled, angular face of the seventeen-year-old girl who had walked over the Heath with him all those years ago was more rounded, more mature and beautiful, with that glow of prospective motherhood.

'Paul, would you be a godfather?' she asked suddenly, smiling at him.

Godfather . . . to Harriet's child . . . when he would give the rest of his life to have been *the father.* Yet the bitter-sweet compliment pleased Paul.

'Of course. I should be honoured, if Tony would not mind.'

'Tony? Oh, he won't mind. He's not very

religious, you know, and to him godparents are just people who send presents at birthdays and Christmas, but it has more spiritual meaning for me. Yes, if it's a boy, I'll call him Paul. It's always been one of my favourite names.'

'No, not Paul!' The words were wrung from the heart of the young Austrian doctor before he could restrain them. Harriet, startled, looked at him.

'Why, Paul? Don't you like your own name?'

'Not much!' he lied swiftly, knowing that the real reason was that he could not bear it. Once he had dreamed of being Harriet's husband, and if she had given him a son, they would have called him Paul. 'It's too ordinary,' he ended lamely.

'Well, I like it,' Harriet said. 'What's your favourite name for a girl, Paul? Because it might be a girl!'

They mentioned one or two, laughing over the more improbable ones. Then Paul asked:

'What about Papa? Hasn't he any preference?'

'Tony? Well, no, not really. I'm afraid this baby isn't a very real person to him yet. He knows it's coming but it has no definite persona for him. I suppose that's common to most fathers, isn't it? They don't have much paternal instinct before the child is born.'

It wasn't a question of paternal instinct, Paul thought but forbore to say. It was just a question of *interest*. The average father-to-be would, in Tony Harley's place, surely have taken more intimate interest in his coming child than this.

Quite suddenly, Paul disliked Harriet's husband as he had never before disliked any man. It wasn't jealousy just because he had married the girl Paul loved. It was the sudden realization that Tony was quite unworthy of her. All afternoon Paul had fought against this belief . . . tried to see his handsome, casual host through Harriet's uncritical eyes; tried not to see his indifferent behaviour towards his wife. There was no tenderness in Tony Harley's voice, no concern for her; nothing but ceaseless, thoughtless demands on her time and attention. How *could* Harriet love such a man? *Did she really love him?* Was she really happy with a worthless, selfish playboy, who openly boasted that he spent as little time in his office as he could?

Paul could not ask her . . . dared not do so. Harriet wanted him to believe in her happiness. Not by a single word had she hinted otherwise. It was only the sixth sense that Paul sometimes possessed about people, warning him that all was not quite well in that household. As a young boy, Paul had been trained to be on his guard with the most friendly, charming men who might be 'quislings', the enemy disguised, spying on him and his mother. That caution had never left

100

him. He always knew when a patient was shamming illness or pain. Knew, too, when a woman about to have a child was concealing her fear. Why was it then that he could not feel any certainty that Harriet was happy? Outwardly she seemed so and much in love with her husband. Was it, he wondered, his dislike of Tony that coloured his opinion, and bred this doubt about their marital happiness?

'Paul, you haven't spoken for five minutes. A penny for your thoughts!' Harriet's low, charming voice interrupted his reverie.

'I was thinking about you, Harriet . . . and your baby!' he answered truthfully.

Harriet smiled.

'It is so nice to have you back in my life, dear Paul. I don't think I ever realized before how much I needed a really good man friend. Of course, Tony and I know dozens of people . . . hundreds, I suppose. But somehow I've never made any really close friends, except the odd girl-friend down here. You're different, somehow. With you I can be myself and feel at ease. I don't feel any need to pretend.' She smiled again, wistfully this time. 'I never did have to pretend with you, Paul, did I? Remember our first meeting? I was hating that Highbury ball so much . . . wishing myself a thousand miles away. I knew I was bound sooner or later to do and say the wrong thing. But with you, somehow it was all right. You were very kind to me, you know. You put the

101

ALAMEDA FREE LIBRARY

gauche schoolgirl quite at her ease.'

I fell in love with you! Paul thought. *From that very first moment, I was in love with you . . . the real you.*

'I liked you just as you were,' he said aloud, striving to keep the conversation on a casual note. 'A shy, awkward little girl who has grown into a very beautiful, poised young woman, I might say.'

'Not so little, and still a bit gawky!' Harriet said, with a laugh. 'Otherwise I admit I'm not the Harriet you first met, Paul. I realize now how stupid I must have seemed then. As to being beautiful now . . . well, you are being, as always, very gallant!' She smiled. 'You forget I have a husband who tells me the truth, and expectant Mamas are hardly beautiful or poised. He finds me most unattractive!'

If he walks in now, I'll knock him down, Paul thought violently. Did Harriet realize what she was saying? That her husband could let her feel anything less than lovely while she carried his child seemed monstrous to Paul, the idealist. Even if the fellow hated the signs of pregnancy, he could at least have let Harriet believe herself lovely in his eyes. But she seemed to take Tony's attitude for granted!

'To me expectant mothers are very beautiful!' said Paul firmly. 'To me, they are at their most beautiful at such a time.'

'Ah, but you're a doctor, Paul! You see things differently. Naturally, in my state, I'd

102

like to agree with you but I don't expect Tony to find me attractive just now. He'll be happier when it's all over and I look more like the girl he married!'

It isn't a wife Harley wants . . . it's a mistress! Paul told himself in disgust. And there were many men like this one. What rankled, hurt, amazed the young Austrian doctor was that Harriet should love Tony. Could she not see for herself how shallow he was? How worthless?

Perhaps I'm being unfair, Paul tried to calm his emotions. *Jealousy is making me exaggerate everything. Tony is probably a nice enough fellow in his own way.*

But Paul was to find out later that his instincts had been right after all.

*   *   *

On the way home in the train on Sunday evening, Eileen said:

'Paul, I don't want to criticize your friends, but I know you have never met Harriet's husband before this weekend, so may I say what's on my mind?'

Paul gave her a quick, surprised look and nodded his head. Eileen was not usually so serious.

'Well, you remember he took me to the pub at Witley last evening? On the way home, he tried to make a pass at me. I'm pretty used to

103

having passes flung by hopeful medical students, as you know, but honestly, Paul, I draw the line at married men, especially when their wives are in Harriet's condition and more especially when I like her as much as I do. I think there's something awfully brave about that girl.'

Paul sat silently, his face stony, his hands clenched in his lap.

'Was it just a bit of fooling, Eileen?'

She shook her head.

'There wasn't any question of misconstruing his motives, Paul. He plied me with gin. As a matter of fact, I do like gin in small quantities now and again, but he had more than a few himself. Then, when we got into the car to drive back, he put his arm round me and kissed me before I could stop him. And it was a *kiss*. I'm telling you. Naturally I told him to stop it. I thought he might be just a bit tight. He just laughed and drove off towards the cottage, then he stopped again before we reached the gate.'

'And then?' Paul prompted Eileen, for clearly she was not enjoying giving him this account, but she seemed to want to make him her confidant.

'Well, he said he wanted a cigarette and lit one. Then he started to ask me about myself . . . where my home was in Ireland and that kind of thing. He was sober enough then, so I sat talking to him. Then he asked me about

104

you; whether we meant anything to each other.' She gave a nervous laugh. 'I said we were good friends and Tony laughed and said: "Not having an affair?" Paul, this is really very embarrassing!'

'Go on!' Paul said in a low voice.

'Well, I told him of course not, and that that wasn't the kind of relationship I had with a man unless I happened to love him. He laughed again and told me it was high time I learnt a few of the facts of life I clearly hadn't learned in my hospital. Then he said . . .' she paused, the colour rushing into her face as she recalled it . . . 'he said he'd be delighted to be the one to teach me and that girls of my age ought to have sex experience, that I was old fashioned and that the average man found a girl far more attractive if she was willing to meet him on his own ground, so to speak.'

'I see!' said Paul. 'Then what?'

'Oh, I got furious and told him what I thought of him and his proposal, but he must have thought I was just playing hard to get. He tried to get hold of and kiss me, so I slapped his face. Even that didn't seem to bring him to his senses. He just said he liked my Irish spirit and that he'd be seeing me again when he was in London; when he hadn't a wife waiting on the doorstep. Paul, I never want to see Anthony Harley again . . . never. He disgusted me.'

'My God!' Paul said, his voice choking.

105

'Poor Harriet . . . Poor, poor Harriet.'

Eileen stared at him. She read the pain in his eyes. It hurt her. She loved Paul von Murren. But she was not lacking in courage. She swallowed her own disappointment and thought only of him.

'You're still in love with Harriet, aren't you, Paul?' she said quietly.

'Yes!' Paul's answer was definite and full of despair. 'But there isn't a thing in the world I can do about it.'

Pity for him . . . for Harriet . . . destroyed any selfish interest Eileen had in Paul. In its place came a great desire to comfort and help him. But she sat there silent and helpless. She knew that Paul was right. There wasn't a thing in the world that either of them could do about it.

CHAPTER SEVEN

Harriet suffered great pain.

For two whole days she was only half-conscious of what went on around her. She knew that Paul had been to see her several times, as well as Eileen.

Lying now in the high, hospital bed this bleak January morning her mind and body dissolved into a delightful vacuum of peace and emptiness. She thought of the tiny helpless

106

body of her baby, her little girl, snug in her cot in the infants' room at the end of the corridor. She felt a new surge of love for her and a new gratitude towards Paul. But for his introduction to Mr Barrow, who had attended the difficult delivery, she knew that she might have lost her baby.

Her mind wandered back to the start of her labour. Tony had been with her in their mews house when the first pains came in the early hours of the morning.

'I think I'd better get to the hospital,' she told him when reluctantly she roused him.

'What *now*?' Tony asked, his voice thick with sleep. He'd been out drinking with some of his friends that evening and had a fiendish headache.

'Well, my pains do seem to be fairly regular,' Harriet said. 'I'm sorry, darling.'

'Surely babies don't arrive so quickly? Can't it wait till morning?' he growled, fuddled with the drink—not quite responsible.

Harriet hesitated. She supposed he was right. She might, after all, be in a panic unnecessarily. Mr Barrow had told her there might be several false alarms. It seemed awful to drag Tony out at this unholy hour—and on a wet winter's night. He hadn't been in bed more than a couple of hours. Maybe it *could* wait till morning . . .

'Go back to sleep, Tony!' she said. 'I'll see how things go.'

In the darkness, she heard Tony's deep, heavy breathing and felt very alone. She hadn't expected him to understand what she was feeling but she wished he had stayed awake to share this vigil with her. She looked at the luminous dial of her bedside clock and tried to time her pains. They weren't very bad or very frequent. She tried to sleep but her mind was too alert, her sensation of alarm inevitable.

An hour passed. The clock hands showed three o'clock. Tired, but unable to sleep, Harriet got up and went down to the kitchen to make herself a cup of tea. Once up, she decided to dress and be ready for the moment when she *must* wake Tony and make him drive her to the hospital. As she pulled on her stockings, she was suddenly doubled over with a new pain, a different one . . . far more severe. It left her gasping. It frightened her too. But still she could not bring herself to disturb her sleeping husband. She told herself this was probably caused by the exertion of dressing.

But another pain followed and on an impulse, she went back to the bedroom and shook Tony awake.

He opened bloodshot eyes and muttered:

'For heaven's sake, Harriet, can't you make up your mind? Either it's coming or it isn't! If you aren't sure, why don't you ring up your doctor friend? He'll know.'

Paul. Yes, she would phone *Paul.*

The moment she got through on his private

108

number and she heard his calm voice questioning her, her panic subsided.

'You're to come in immediately, Harriet, do you understand? There's nothing to be alarmed about but I want you here at once. I'll let Barrow know. We'll be ready for you.'

So Tony had to get up and drive her to the hospital. Paul stood at the reception-desk awaiting them.

'Think I should hang around?' Tony asked. He looked unkempt and Paul, who shot him a quick glance, saw that he was hungover. He said abruptly:

'No! You can't do any good . . . unless Harriet would like you to stay.'

Harriet quickly rejected the idea and told her husband to go back to bed and get some more sleep. Then another severe pain doubled her up. A nurse helped her along the corridor to the labour ward. Mr Barrow appeared on the scene later. For a few moments Paul was alone with her, holding one of her hot, damp hands in his cool firm ones.

'Eileen's on night duty this week so I've fixed with Matron for her to look after you, Harriet. I thought you might like to have her.'

She smiled at him gratefully. He must have guessed how frightened and alone she was feeling now.

'Barrow and Eileen are getting scrubbed up. You'll be in the very best hands so you've nothing to worry about.'

'Paul, I don't want to make a fuss but isn't there something I could have for this pain?'

'Yes, darling, there is!' Somehow in the stress of that moment, the endearment had slipped past him and went almost unnoticed. 'You'll be given an injection as soon as you're downstairs.'

'Paul, can't you stay with me?'

'Yes, if Barrow wants me, I'll be there.'

Yet for the first time in his experience, Paul knew that he did not want to assist at this birth. He wondered if his nerves could stand the sight of Harriet's confinement. He was well aware of the complication Barrow expected. It would not be a really dangerous birth but complicated.

Later, however, in his white sterilized gown and mask, in the labour ward where he had delivered so many babies, Paul no longer looked on Harriet as a person . . . only as a patient. He stood beside her, talking to her, telling her what was happening, what would happen next, calming her.

Once Wilfred Barrow said in an undertone:

'Wish she'd come in an hour sooner . . .'

In the dim mists confusing her, she whispered:

'Sorry . . . didn't want to disturb my husband . . . wasn't sure . . .' Then she drifted away again under the influence of a deeper anaesthetic.

When Harriet came round, she found

herself in her hospital bed; Paul was beside her. Still semi-conscious she asked for her baby. Eileen brought the little bundle to her.

'A boy?' Harriet asked.

'No, a girl!' Paul told her gently. 'She's very pretty, Harriet . . . just like you.'

Harriet smiled and drifted back to sleep.

Since then, she had lain here, terribly tired. Not only physically but mentally she felt this great fatigue. Eileen who was her 'special' was wonderful to her . . . gentle, kind, attentive. Paul came often to see her. Yesterday, when she asked him about the birth, he had told her how nearly she had lost her infant. She asked him then if she could have other children.

'Of course, Harriet. Barrow did a truly wonderful job, you know. And next time, you won't, I hope, suffer in the same way.'

'You saw your god-daughter being born?' she asked him.

Paul nodded. He was deeply moved by the memory.

'Yes, I did. And I congratulate you, Harriet, both on her arrival and your courage. You were very brave.'

'I wasn't really afraid with you there,' Harriet said dreamily. 'How good you were to me, Paul!'

'Well, you're to take things very easy for a while,' Paul said, using his doctor's voice to hide his personal feelings. 'No visitors for a day or two!'

111

'Not even Tony?'

'Yes, of course the proud Papa can come.'

But somehow Tony's visits seemed to tire Harriet. He was so full of energy and high spirits. Even when he first saw her and his daughter he was only interested in the baby for a moment, then began to describe the celebration he would have with 'the boys', and discussed plans for a big party when she came out of hospital.

Harriet's heart sank at the prospect of a big party.

She did not know it, but always after Tony's visits her temperature went up. Mr Barrow, noting this, was tempted to refuse Tony admittance. He consulted Paul, who hesitated, fearing that he might act from motives of personal jealousy and dislike for the man. He suggested Barrow should warn Tony that Harriet needed extreme quiet if she was to be able to feed her child.

Tony continued to arrive at the hospital daily, with armfuls of flowers and fruit. Paul, hearing these gifts were brought by Harriet's husband, tried to think better of the man. But he had no notion of Tony's duplicity. He came daily to see his wife because Eileen was now on day duty, and Tony wanted to further his brief acquaintance with her. Her reluctance to respond to his advances down at Witley had ignited his desire to conquer the pretty, fair-haired nurse.

Eileen knew what he was up to. Taking the flowers or fruit from him, he would detain her and make her answer irrelevant questions about Harriet and the child. Then he would ask her to change her mind and say she'd attend the celebration party he was having when Harriet got home.

'After all, Eileen, you've been nursing her. She'll want you to be there,' he argued.

Eileen had a curt reply for such attempts, but could not bring herself to tell Paul. He looked so tired and worried. She knew that he was wretched. What good could it do to further his dislike of Harriet's husband? She was afraid now that she ought never to have told him in the first place about Tony's behaviour down in Witley. It must be unbearable for a man to see the woman he loved not only married to such a man, but giving birth to his child.

Paul did not confide in Eileen the extent of his tortured thoughts. Only to his mother did he write the truth. They had always been close. He needed the balm of her wisdom—her calm, loving advice.

Should I stop seeing Harriet, Mutti? (he had written). *I know she needs my friendship and I want more than anything in the world to be able to make life a little happier for her. I know it is wrong to love another man's wife yet I can't wipe out a*

113

love that has been with me all my life. Harriet means more to me than anything in the world. The man she has married is as unworthy of her as any man could be. What shall I do, Mutti dear? She may need a good friend if ever she should discover what her husband is really like. I love her so desperately . . .

In Austria the *Gräfin* von Murren read this despairing cry from her son's heart. She was a fine woman with a deep understanding of human nature. She knew that it would be useless to suggest her son should stamp on his feelings for this English girl. He had already shown himself far too constant in that direction. Nonetheless it worried her deeply that Paul, her splendid son, should waste himself on a love that could, as he admitted, never be returned. Why must he waste his life over unrequited passion? The *Gräfin* had wanted something so different for Paul . . . a happy marriage to a nice girl who could help him in his work, give him the children he so much wanted.

But Paul had asked for her counsel and she strove hard to find the right answer for him. Finally, after sleepless nights, she wrote back to him:

My dearest,
You will know without my telling you

how unhappy I am for you in this predicament. I do not question your behaviour. You must obviously have been a great comfort and help to your Harriet. But, my son, I feel I must tell you that I believe for you to go on seeing her is only to store up trouble for yourself and unhappiness for her, too. You see, Paul, if you have correctly judged this man she has married, can you not also see that she must eventually compare him with yourself. That she has not already done so is probably due to the fact that she has been concerned with her child. To lose your friendship and comfort would distress her but at least she will not have learned that she has lost the better man . . . and discover that she still loves you.

You must try not to see her too often. I know this will be hard, perhaps the more so because of the truth you learned about her mother's conduct. How any woman could do such a thing to her own daughter is beyond me, and I am appalled to think how much unnecessary suffering she has inflicted upon you both.

However, it can do no good to waste time on regrets and what might have been. One must look forward not back, and, Paul, I cannot see any peace of mind, or happiness, if you go on as you are. Once you are sure Harriet is well, and as happy

*as circumstances allow, I beg you to put an
end to these visits you continually pay her.*

Paul knew with a wretched feeling of
certainty as he read her letter that his mother
was right. The more devotion he expended
upon Harriet the more Tony might suffer by
comparison. At least she still had her illusions
about her husband. She might even keep them
for she was so young still, so generous. That
she had found Tony out in one infidelity Paul
did not know. Neither did he know that she
had made up her mind to forgive, forget and
trust him absolutely.

Paul tried to do as his mother wished and
keep away from Harriet, but the longing to see
her became too much for him—at least while
she was in the hospital. He knew these few
precious hours might be the last he would ever
spend with her. He dared not waste them. And
Harriet was always so pleased to see him, so
touched by the interest he took in her and her
tiny daughter.

'You must have a thousand things to do,
Paul, yet you always manage to spend time
with me.'

'It's for my own pleasure,' he said, knowing
that to love her like this must always be pain as
well as pleasure. There was so much he wanted
to give her and so little that he could. 'It's nice
to get away from hospital routine even if it's
only for a half-hour. I shall miss you when you

116

go.'

'I shall miss you, Paul!' The words were lightly spoken by Harriet, but they sounded like a vast echo inside his heart. 'But you'll come to see us often, won't you?' she added. 'When I leave here it won't mean we shan't see each other if not quite so often. You do value our friendship, don't you?'

He walked quickly over to the window and stared out, hoping she could not see his despairing face.

'Of course. But it won't always be easy to get away, Harriet, much as I should wish to. I am usually so busy, here. When I am not actually on duty, I *should* be studying.'

Harriet laughed.

'Oh, Paul! You were always a glutton for work. I suppose I shouldn't be keeping you from it now! You'll be glad to get me out of here.'

'No!' The words were wrung from him. 'I hate to think you are leaving so soon now.'

'Dear Paul!' Harriet said quietly. 'But we will see each other from time to time. It is inconceivable that we should lose each other again after all these years.'

Yes, how fully he agreed with that and yet how could he explain to her that he *must* stop seeing her without hurting her, without giving away the true reasons?

He tried to dissemble.

'Of course, Harriet, I'll come down to see

117

you whenever I have time but you must not expect it to be often. You are going to continue living at Henry VIII?'

Harriet nodded.

'I don't believe London is a good place in which to bring up a child,' she said. 'But we'll keep on our house in Elvin Mews because Tony won't want to bury himself in the country for good. He thrives on a hectic social life. I suppose in some ways we're very unsuited! Yet we manage to be happy together.'

'Perhaps you complement one another,' Paul said with difficulty. 'I've no doubt you're the steadying influence, Harriet, and that Tony, in turn, jollies you out of your inclinations to be a hermit.'

'I don't think I ever mind being alone,' Harriet said thoughtfully. 'I got used to it as a child. My mother was always out and when I was with my father he was so quiet it was almost like being alone. I do so often wish he were still alive, Paul. We were such good friends and I think he would have been delighted with his first grandchild.'

Paul stayed grimly silent. He knew—for she had told him—that her mother had cabled congratulations from Jamaica, where she was sun-seeking with her new young husband. The cable had been followed by a letter, typical of Lucy, openly hating the idea of being made a grandmother.

'You have decided on a name for the baby?'

118

Paul asked suddenly.

'Tony doesn't seem fussy although he likes the idea of calling her Antonia. I think we'll probably agree on that. It's flattering to him—the feminine of Anthony. You know, I have to keep reminding myself that she is a girl. I was so certain she'd be a boy and that we'd call him Paul.'

The doctor turned away from her again, afraid, as always, that she might read his expression. *He* had been glad the baby was a girl. The idea of Harriet calling her son Paul, the son who would not have been his flesh and blood, was intolerable.

'I suppose my mother won't see her for another month,' Harriet went on. 'I haven't set eyes on her for ages. She's been so much abroad.'

'She's just got married again, hasn't she?' Paul forced himself to be polite about Lucy, wondering how he could so hate the mother and yet love the daughter so well.

'Yes, she married Bernard Maybury just before Christmas. In her last letter she said she was divinely happy. I wonder if she will ever know genuine happiness.'

And Harriet sighed. Somehow the idea of her mother's marriage with that long-haired, effeminate young man with whom she had become infatuated after Rex went out of her life was utterly abhorrent to Harriet. The thought of her mother also brought back the

119

reminder of what she had done to her and Paul eight years ago. She ought to hate her. Yet now that Paul was back in her life as a close and dear friend again, it did not seem to matter so much. After all, had it not been for that break between her and Paul, she would never have married Tony, and without Tony there would have been no Antonia. She adored her pretty, blue-eyed baby.

'I can't wait to have her home all to myself!' she spoke her thoughts aloud. 'I seem to see so little of her here!'

'That is because you still aren't very strong and you need lots of rest,' Paul said. 'You must remember, Harriet, that you had a rather bad time of it. You want building up once you get home. You say you will have help with the housework but you intend to look after Antonia yourself.'

'Yes, oh yes!' said Harriet.

'Will your husband mind you always having to be there to feed her and so on?'

'No—he is being charming about it—quite keen, in fact, for me to look after Antonia myself,' said the innocent Harriet.

Paul pursed his lips, wondering if Master Tony was not brewing fresh mischief and seizing every excuse to keep his wife occupied while he fooled around.

'Oh, well—you must have a good tonic.' Paul trod on his thoughts and forced the words.

'Yes, Doctor!' Harriet said demurely. He was right. The one time she had been out of bed, she had felt desperately weak. She slept a great deal of the day as if she could not get enough of it.

I wish I could be the one to go home with her, Paul thought with a longing that ached through his whole body. *I'd like to be there to take care of her, nurse her back to health, keep her always as happy as she is now. What will happen to her when she gets back? Will Tony be there? Will he be irritable, restless? Will he tire her? I shall never have a moment's peace of mind until I know she is all right . . . yet I cannot go on seeing her.*

Eileen, he thought suddenly. Perhaps he could persuade Eileen to keep in touch with Harriet for him. At least then he would have news of her occasionally which would save him from needless worry. Perhaps it was stupid of him to worry at all. Perhaps the responsibilities of fatherhood would make a different man of Tony. If only Paul could believe that! But somehow, he knew that Harriet's husband was not the type to face up to domestic difficulties. The crying of a baby could be the most irritating noise or the most appealing. Babies' tiny garments airing round the fire could be the most touching or an offensive sight. Paul's work had taken him into many homes both in this country and abroad. He had come up against both types of husband. And try as he

121

might, he could not see Tony being domesticated.

Why, *why* did Harriet marry him? Because she was lonely? Because she wanted children? Or out of physical infatuation? It could not be because she had loved him. But Paul could not ask her. On the face of things she seemed content.

*   *   *

But his heart was full of foreboding on the day that Tony—playing his part that day, at least—drove his wife and two-week-old daughter away from the hospital. For the rest of that day Paul worked with a grim face and tight-shut mouth. Only Eileen knew the reason—and pitied him.

CHAPTER EIGHT

The party was in full swing. The Harleys' small, elegant mews house was crowded with people, laughing, talking, drinking. Harriet tried to see through the smoky haze towards Tony, where he stood dispensing drinks at the tiny cocktail bar he had recently bought. He was in the best of spirits, and tired though she was, Harriet was happy that he should be so proud of his little daughter. Antonia had been shown to all the guests.

It compensated for the criticism he had made earlier about her figure.

'You're very thick in the waist still,' he had grumbled, 'and I don't think large breasts suit a tall, slim, boyish figure like yours used to be.'

She had pretended not to mind and did indeed regret the fact that she couldn't wear the tight model dress Tony liked. She had put on a smart new black dress but it didn't really suit her. Her face was thin and sallow, and her hair had lost its lustre. She was certainly not looking her best this evening and was tired all the time.

I wish Paul could have been here, she thought, not for the first time. Except for Eileen, who had come to please her, they were all Tony's friends. She felt curiously remote from them, almost as if she were an unseen ghost watching their antics—feeling almost disdainful of them. It was nearly midnight. The party had begun at eight. Small wonder that she was beginning to feel sleepy and to long for bed. She had slipped away at half past ten to feed Antonia and had nearly fallen asleep while doing so. Although the voices and the blare of the radio-gramophone penetrated the bedroom, the atmosphere was clear there; she felt able to breathe, and in the comfortable glow of the electric fire she held her baby in her arms and began to feel completely detached from that other world outside the door.

Eileen had come in to find her nodding over the baby's downy head. She told Harriet in her best professional manner that she should go to bed.

'Paul was horrified when he heard you were having this party your first day out of hospital!' she said. 'You're not fit enough to cope yet, Harriet.'

'But, Eileen, I'm going down to Witley tomorrow. There wouldn't have been another chance without my dragging Antonia back to London. Tony was so anxious to celebrate with his friends and show off as the proud Papa, I couldn't disappoint him.'

Eileen bit back the unpleasant things she wanted to say about Tony and, taking the baby from Harriet's arms, patted the small bundle on the back. Antonia obliged with a charming cooing sound.

'She *is* sweet, isn't she?' Harriet said as she straightened her dress, all her mother love in her voice. 'You do think she's pretty, don't you, Eileen?'

The young Irish nurse laughed.

'Yes, I do! As a matter of fact, I think she's rather like Tony. She's got his crinkly sort of hair and a wicked smile.'

Harriet smiled too.

'She's been so good tonight, hasn't cried at all. But I don't know how I shall drag myself out of bed to feed her at six, though!'

'Why not put an end to this party now?' Eileen asked. 'Surely you could do it? Tony could tell everyone you're tired.'

'Oh, no!' Harriet said quickly. 'It's only just beginning. I expect people will hang on and dance till all hours. Besides, I'm not really tired, Eileen . . . only sleepy!'

Eileen let the lie pass. There was no point in making an issue of it since Harriet clearly meant this to be Tony's night. Eileen thought how angry Paul would be if she told him. She hadn't really wanted to come but Harriet had begged her, and Paul had been set on it, too.

'You *must* go, Eileen, please. She'll need looking after. I've tried to tell her she should be quiet for a week or two at least but all she says is that she promised Tony. God, I could kill that man! Do go and keep an eye on her, please, Eileen!'

She hadn't been able to refuse him. Her interest in him had taken on a new colour. She felt much more of a sister to him than a would-be girl-friend. Knowing how greatly he loved Harriet Harley had killed Eileen's own half-formed hopes that he might ask her to marry him, and now, in its place, she felt this platonic affection and need to make things easier for him if she could.

'You don't want to get so exhausted you can't feed Antonia, Harriet!' she said warningly, as she put the baby back into her cot. 'This sort of night is the best way to go

125

about it.'

'I'll rest tomorrow!' Harriet said. 'I can go back to bed after the six o'clock feed and sleep till ten. We aren't going down to Henry VIII till after lunch. I'll be all right, Eileen, really.'

But as the evening wore on, Harriet began to feel more and more tired. Once she found Tony and told him she wanted to slip away quietly and go to bed, but he had vetoed the idea instantly.

'You can't possibly disappear now, Harriet. If you do the whole party will break up. Look, have a drink. That'll buck you up.'

But the champagne he forced on her had only made her feel rather sick and dizzy. It was Eileen, watching her from across the room, who was first to see her sway, then fall. Beside her in an instant, she put a pillow beneath Harriet's head and turned to the now silent crowd of onlookers.

'You'd better all go home! Harriet is ill,' she said. 'And will someone open the windows, please? Tony, get me some cold water!'

The crowd, murmuring sympathetically, began to disperse. The party was obviously over. The house emptied.

Tony had had more to drink than was good for him. He brought the glass and his hand shook so that some of the water fell on Harriet's face. She looked up at her husband dazedly.

'So . . . sorry, darling,' she murmured. 'Silly

126

. . . of me . . .

Seeing she was all right, Tony's concern turned to irritation. Eileen's presence prevented him saying how he felt about the best party they'd had in years being brokcn up on this sober note. But it did not prevent him turning on his heel and walking away from Harriet. His steps were none too steady.

Eileen called him back. Her dislike of him crystallized into hatred as she said:

'Help me carry Harriet to bed, please.'

He obeyed, scowling, and left them alone.

Gently, Eileen undressed Harriet, pretending not to see the tears that were sliding quietly down her cheeks. Her professional manner well to the fore, she spoke brusquely and sensibly.

'You'll be all right now. It was just the heat. Unfortunately, I can't stay the night, Harriet, as I am on duty tomorrow morning . . . this morning, I suppose it is. But you are not to get out of your bed till it's time to drive to the cottage. I shall tell Tony he's to bring the baby in to you to feed, then you're to go straight back to sleep. That's an order!'

'Really, I'm quite all right!' Harriet said, but could not stop the tears. 'Please leave me now, Eileen. You'll be so tired in the morning, too, and with all your work—it's a shame. Th . . . thank you . . . f-f . . . for looking after me!'

Eileen fetched her coat.

Tony did not appreciate her tone of voice

127

when she bade him goodnight out in the hall. He shifted uncomfortably as she said:

'Anyone could have seen she wasn't fit enough for a party like this. It's up to you to take care of her, you know. You are her husband. Having a baby . . . especially the way Harriet did . . . can be a very exhausting business and she's far from strong yet.'

'Dash it all, she had two weeks in hospital!'

'Yes, and needed another week. And if you don't watch out she'll be back in hospital for another two weeks, which I don't suppose you particularly want . . . or do you?'

He met the flash of the Irish eyes and his own dropped. To tell the truth, those weeks while Harriet had been away had been quite good fun. He'd been free to come and go as he pleased and there was no one to nag at him if he wanted to go on 'a jag' and drink too much. He'd enjoyed tonight's celebration of the birth of his daughter but now, in more sober mood, he began to see that being a father wasn't all going to be fun.

'Of course I don't want Harriet to go back to hospital,' he said truculently.

'And you'll take the baby to her in the morning. Harriet's not to get out of her bed, do you understand? She's still very weak and she ought to have a nurse.'

Tony agreed in order to put an end to this boring conversation and get Eileen out of the flat. He had no use for Eileen in this mood.

128

Neither had he any intention of getting up to do Harriet's job for her. She'd wanted this kid—let her get on with her motherhood. When he first heard the baby's cry, through a fog of sleep, he told himself it was silly for both of them to be disturbed and since Harriet had got to feed the baby, it wasn't really saving her much to hand her the infant. So he went back to sleep and Harriet, exhausted though she was, heard her baby's continued wail and wearily climbed out of bed. Her legs were shaking, her head whirled.

It never occurred to her to call Tony. Or if it did cross her mind, she rejected the idea quickly, telling herself that it was unfair to wake him. He must be very tired.

But in the end she had to call him. To her deepest concern, and even horror, she found that she had no milk to give the child. The late night and her fainting fit had had the effect of drying up the supply.

In a panic, Harriet went across and shook Tony's shoulders.

'What shall I do?' she asked helplessly, talking above the baby's hungry screams. 'I never thought to ask Eileen for a formula. Tony, please wake up. *Please!*'

And tears of weakness, so common to women after the birth of a baby, began to flow. She could not check them. Tony looked up at her from his rumpled pillow with obvious distaste.

129

'What in heaven's name is wrong *now*, Harriet?'

'I can't feed Antonia. I can't feed her!' Harriet cried, struggling to control her rising hysteria as the baby's cries rose in volume.

Tony did not trouble to conceal his annoyance.

'For God's sake, Harriet, surely they taught you what to do in hospital?'

'But I could feed her then. Now I haven't anything to give her,' Harriet said on a sob. 'What am I to do, Tony?'

'Perhaps if you start by getting that screaming kid into another room we can discuss it,' Tony said, his own head bursting.

Harriet quickly placed the now scarlet threshing infant into her carrycot and carried it into the sitting-room. When she came back to Tony he was almost asleep again.

He muttered at her: 'Phone that nurse, Eileen. She'll cope.

'I can't, Tony. She'll be asleep and she's on duty today,' began Harriet.

But Tony was asleep again. Her sudden amazement that he could just abandon her and his hungry baby shocked her back to calmness. She wouldn't ring Eileen, but she could ring Paul who was on night duty. Eileen had said so. Why, oh why hadn't she thought of asking about emergency feeding before she left the hospital?

It took a few moments for the hospital to

130

find Paul. The relief of hearing his voice was so enormous that Harriet was near to tears again.

'Paul, I feel such a fool. I don't know what to do.' She explained briefly what had happened.

'I'm not surprised,' was Paul's comment. 'But don't be too upset, my dear. You'll probably be back to normal once you get some rest. Meanwhile, have you a baby's bottle in the place?'

'No, I haven't,' Harriet said wretchedly. 'I have one down at Witley but I never thought this might happen while I was here. I haven't any baby food either.'

There was a moment's silence. Then Paul said:

'Send Tony round in a taxi or by car. I'll have everything ready waiting for him.'

He, in turn, waited while Harriet remained quiet.

'What's the matter?' he asked at last. 'Isn't Tony there?'

'Y-yes,' Harriet admitted wretchedly. 'It's just that he . . . he's asleep and . . .'

'You mean he had too much to drink at the party and isn't willing to get up.' Paul could not resist the sharp accusation. Then, remembering that Tony was Harriet's husband, he tried to ease the situation for her.

'I'll come round myself, Harriet,' he said. 'I'll just let night Sister and my assistant know I shall be gone for half an hour. Meanwhile, don't worry if Antonia cries. She won't starve . . . not if she goes without for three days, so a few hours won't hurt her. Just grin and bear it till I get there.'

'Paul, I can't drag you out. I'll come for the stuff myself . . .'

'You'll do nothing of the kind. You'll stay there. Have some hot water ready boiled. That's all we'll need.'

An hour later Paul was there, looking across the disordered drawing-room at Harriet and trying not to see how deathly white and tired she looked.

'See, there's nothing to worry about now,' he said comfortingly, as she removed the empty bottle from the baby's mouth and laid her back in her cot. 'You must go back to bed and get some sleep, my dear.'

But instead, as he had feared might happen, Harriet burst into tears . . . tears of relief as much as fatigue. As he put his arms around her, it was an agony almost beyond bearing to have her there yet knowing that next door lay her sleeping husband; knowing he could never speak of his overwhelming desire to keep her in his arms, to love her and take care of her always.

'Oh, Paul, you're so good to me. I am so sorry to be such a stupid little idiot.' She sniffed like a small girl into the handkerchief he gave her. 'It's awful to have dragged you out at this time of the morning.'

'You should be back in bed,' Paul said, releasing her arms which still clung to him, not in love, as he well knew, but in need of the comfort he offered her. If his voice was abrupt, almost cool in tone, it was only to hide his inner emotions, but Harriet felt suddenly self-conscious and ashamed.

No wonder if Paul thought she was a fool. No wonder, too, if he was annoyed at being brought out at this time of the night . . . or morning. He probably felt, and rightly, that Tony should have come for the things she needed—Tony, who was still snoring gently in their bedroom.

She was suddenly wretchedly ashamed of her husband. She hated to have him shown up in such a bad light before Paul—Paul, who was so worthwhile, so very good to her, so thoughtful of others. His opinion of Tony and of her must be a very poor one.

'Paul, I'm so sorry . . .' she began helplessly. But he broke in again, his voice still hard, almost bitter:

'Stop saying that, Harriet: it's the third time in less than an hour.' He tried not to see the hurt expression in her eyes, nor notice the flush of colour that stained her white cheeks. 'Now I really must get back.'

'Let me get you a cup of tea before you go, Paul.'

He turned on her then, his quite unbearable

133

love for her making him cruel in his violence.

'Harriet, will you stop being so confoundedly thoughtful of other people and start thinking of yourself for once in a while. Or if you won't think of yourself, think of your baby. You need rest and sleep—lots and lots of it. Now go back to bed. Oh, God, Harriet . . .' His voice broke into a horrified tenderness as he saw the tears rush back to her eyes. He no longer knew, nor cared, that she didn't belong to him, that he had no right ever to let her know his feelings. All that mattered to him was that he had hurt her, however involuntarily. He, Paul, had made her cry.

'Harriet . . . my darling, my darling. Don't. Please, my love, don't cry. I can't stand to see you unhappy.'

She was in his arms now, sobbing uncontrollably against his shoulder. She heard his words, the endearments, through the fog of weeping that enveloped her and knew a quick and wonderful joy in what he said. He wasn't angry, wasn't disapproving. He loved her, *still loved her.*

For a moment she stood silently in his embrace, unable to draw away, unable to stop him speaking the words she had never expected to hear, never for one moment imagined she might so want to hear from any other man but Tony.

'Harriet, I love you—so much I can't stand seeing you so unhappy. You mean more to me

134

than anything in the whole world.'

'Oh, Paul!' The words were wrung from the depth of her being. It was a kind of involuntary surrender of herself and her need into his keeping. Then, quite suddenly, like a shock of cold water, she realized what was happening; remembered that she was Tony's wife, here in their home only half dressed and in Paul's arms.

Paul, too, was remembering and was appalled at his loss of control. As she drew away from him he stared at her slim, drooping shoulders, aghast at what he had done.

'You must try to forgive me—to forget what I said,' he spoke at last into the painful silence that followed. His voice was now distant, formal, even cold. 'I'm afraid I was going back to the past for a while. I'd forgotten that you— you and Tony . . .'

He broke off but she filled the gap for him, sensing his pain and longing to help him.

'I know you didn't really mean what you said, Paul. You were just trying to . . . to comfort me. It was all my fault for being so weak. I don't seem able to stop crying these days.'

'That's just natural,' Paul said, speaking once again as a doctor. 'You'll find it'll wear off in time. You must try to get plenty of rest in the country. It's tomorrow you go, isn't it?'

'Today!' she corrected him with an attempted smile.

135

She guessed he was trying to avoid any mention of his sudden admission of love for her. As he continued to speak coolly and impersonally, she found it hard to believe he had actually voiced his feelings. Only after he had left, not touching her hand but going abruptly without more than a brief good-bye, did she allow herself to consider that Paul had admitted his love for her, a love which had lasted all these years. And she had been glad, selfishly glad, to hear it. It had, in fact, been a moment of quite unbearable joy. Yet why should she feel this way when she was in love with Tony? When for years she had loved Tony not Paul.

But try as she might, she could not find an answer to her self-questioning. She would not admit to more than a great need of Paul, of his friendship, his gentleness, his understanding. To admit she might still love him was so filled with appalling complications, that some inner sense forbade even the recognition of her true state of mind. She believed sincerely that she still loved the man she had married, despite his faults, despite his lack of sympathy and understanding.

Harriet had taken her marriage vows with utmost sincerity, believing that she would go on loving Tony for better and for worse as long as she lived. If sometimes the 'worse' seemed so much more in evidence, she did not criticize or blame him, for she realized that Tony could never be different. Only once had she contemplated divorce—when she learned Tony had been unfaithful to her. But then it had been the instant reaction of someone deeply hurt and shocked, and she had forgiven him and stayed with him, even if for a while her love for him had been in abeyance.

She was blind to most of his faults because she chose to be so. She didn't want her marriage to break up and now she dared not start to compare Tony with Paul for fear of what she would find. But she could not avoid thinking about Paul's declaration of love. The first joy in hearing it turned quickly to pain as she realized the implications. She could never belong to Paul . . . never. Because she had nothing to offer him it would be unfair to go on taking from him as she now realized she had been doing. Perhaps, were it not for meeting her again, something might have come of his friendship with Eileen. Paul so deserved a good wife . . . someone to love him and care for him. She must not ever again ask him to come to her. However much she might need his friendship, she must subjugate her feelings for his sake.

But as sleep and exhaustion enveloped her, she knew a sudden deep and appalling sadness at the thought of losing him. It had been hard enough the first time . . . those many years ago. But it hurt as much again now, for despite her arguments, she knew she was profoundly glad

137

of Paul's enduring love.

*   *   *

Paul, however, was far from sleep. He sat at his desk, medical books and magazines pushed to one side, as he strove to write the most difficult letter of his life. He knew he had to write to Harriet; to offer some explanation of his behaviour; knew, too, that he would not be able to see her again. For however much this letter convinced her he had not really meant what he had said, he feared he might give himself away each and every time he was near her.

Oh, Harriet, my darling, he thought. If it would help you to be sure of my love, then I would never try to deny it. But if ever you should come to feel more than a friendly need of me, perhaps even to love me again, what happiness could there be for either of us?

He pulled himself up short at this stage of his thoughts, for he dared not think that Harriet, though she might not know it, could still be a little in love with him. He had found it nearly impossible to believe she should love a man like Tony, yet even now, she appeared not to see her husband for the man he really was.

Paul dragged his thoughts back to the paper in front of him and tried again to find the right words.

138

At last his pen began to move across the page, slowly at first, but more speedily as the lies came following on one after another.

My dear Harriet,

I expect you have been wondering what can have possessed me to speak as I did to you. When you hear the truth, I am afraid you will no longer wish to call me one of your friends. The fact is, Harriet, that it is such a long time since I held an attractive woman in my arms . . . in her dressing-gown at that, that I was quite carried away by baser instincts. I see now how very wrong I was to take advantage of your sweetness, your need of a friendly shoulder to cry on, the more wrong because you contacted me as a doctor and I should never allow such thoughts to cross my mind about a patient. But I forgot at the time that we were not on the footing that had existed eight years ago.

I am the more ashamed because I feel guilty not only towards you but towards Eileen, whom, as you've no doubt guessed, I fully intend to marry one day. I beg you not to mention what happened to her and to try to forgive me and forget what kind of man I am.

I am, as always, your friend and admirer,
Paul von Murren.

As he folded the letter and placed it in an envelope, Paul had the feeling that he had really burned his boats at last. Harriet could never believe he loved her after this, and would never even wonder if she had been mistaken now that he had told her he loved Eileen. She would be ashamed of his weakness and possibly even despise him for it.

With a twisted smile Paul told himself that he had really made himself out to be the kind of man to whom she was already married. Well, that at least would forbid any unfavourable comparisons between them. He knew he could never hope to see her again, could not bear to see the reproach that must surely be in her eyes.

But as he stamped the letter and pushed it away from him with loathing he felt almost relieved. For one blessed moment he had been able to tell her of his love. For a short while, at least, she would believe in it. Wrong though it had been of him, the expression of his feelings after so many years was as if some clamp over his heart, some ever-present pain, had been temporarily relieved. It would come back, he knew, perhaps with greater intensity, for he would never cease loving her; never have a moment's peace wondering if she was happy, well, in need of him. As to his marrying Eileen—well, that would never happen. He would remain single all his life, since he could never have the woman he loved.

'Oh, Harriet, Harriet!' He whispered her name aloud. 'If I could only have married you when we were both so young, so much in love! I would have made you happy—I would have taken such care of you . . .'

And for the first time in his life, Paul's career had no meaning for him, was no compensation for what he had lost. With Harriet, he would have had everything. Without her his ambition, his work, his life, was meaningless.

Despairingly, he covered his face with his long, sensitive fingers, and gave way to the utter hopelessness that enveloped his heart.

CHAPTER NINE

Antonia was two months old. The first new-born wrinkled look had long since gone and to Harriet she seemed the prettiest baby in the world. She loved her passionately, with all the pent-up longing of her ardent nature that had never really, until now, had a channel of expression. With Tony, she had had to learn to curb her emotions and to teach herself to conceal her sentiments and her sensitivity. Except in bed, Tony did not like her to express affection for him.

But with the baby she could love her as much as she wished . . . too much, perhaps, to be good for Harriet. Her whole being was now concentrated on Antonia, to the exclusion of all other feeling.

If Paul's letter had had something to do with this passionate interest in her child, Harriet did not know it. As he had surmised, the letter shocked her deeply. Somehow she had never thought of Paul as being a prey to his physical needs. Nor would she have believed that he could be attracted to one woman while being in love with another. Because she had always had such a high opinion of him, Harriet tried to change that first shock by making excuses for him. It had been as much her fault, calling him out in the early hours of the morning, throwing herself into his arms only half dressed. She felt the colour rising to her cheeks every time she remembered how thoughtlessly and shamelessly she had behaved. Thoughtlessly, since at the time she had no tiny particle of thought for attracting Paul. Selfishly, she had been far too engrossed in her distress and her need of his help.

While she could not bring herself to think any the worse of him, she was deeply upset and she knew that it would be best for them both not to meet again. The old easy comradeship could never be re-established after what had happened. They would both be far too conscious of what had passed between them. She had been very distressed—far more than she believed possible, for she had had no idea

142

until then how much she had come to depend on Paul's friendship.

Some inner instinct prompting her to do the right thing, she had tried to turn to Tony for what Paul had offered her, for the understanding and sympathy and help he had given her during those weeks in hospital. But Tony, at least consistent in his behaviour, had been quite unresponsive. Harriet's preoccupation with the baby had irritated him almost as much as the child's cries had done. Admittedly, Harriet was able to feed Antonia again within two days of being down at the cottage, but nonetheless the baby always seemed to be crying about something and, in that small house, it was impossible to ignore the fact. Tony was restless and bored and Harriet's continued expectation of his interest in his small daughter began to get on his nerves.

'Dash it all, Harriet, you can't really expect me to feel very much for her at this stage. She does nothing but eat and sleep and cry! Why can't you get a good nurse who knows how to cope with her and then we can go back to London!'

'But, Tony, she's *my* baby. I don't want to hand her over to someone else to care for.'

She tried, after that, not to bother him with the baby's needs. She was forced to admit that Tony was not—and perhaps never would be—the kind of father she would have liked for their

143

children. Unhappiness and disappointment marred their first days at the cottage together and Harriet became acutely conscious of Tony's restlessness and boredom with country life. She realized it might mean losing him in so far as he would want to go back to London for at least part of the week, but still she could not bring herself to get a nanny for Antonia.

Wearily, Harriet strove to solve her problem. She knew Tony wanted to come back to her bedroom but, with Antonia's difficult birth and with the tiredness that resulted from feeding her, she did not feel up to coping with Tony's physical demands. Now, however, in an effort to improve their relationship, she submitted to what for her had become no more than a way of pleasing Tony. The consequent loss of sleep yet again had the effect of making her lose her milk.

Wearily Harriet put the baby back on a bottle, but the change did not suit the child, and for a few days she cried almost continually. Harriet took her to the local baby clinic only to be told that she would settle down in due course and that she, Harriet, must not worry.

So exhausted did she become that she felt her nerves to be at breaking point, and it was all she could do not to shout at Tony to leave her alone when he tried again to make love to her. There was little tenderness in his rough demands on her, and she knew that it was partly her own fault, for she could not respond as he wished while half of her mind was listening for the baby's crying. On such an occasion it was not long after midnight when the first wail came and Harriet's nerves tensed.

'God damn it!' Tony cried furiously. 'Can't you forget that child for a moment?'

Harriet tried—tried to give her mind to Tony and *his* need of her, but she could not.

'I'm s . . . sorry!' she whispered into the darkness. 'It's just hearing her . . .' She broke off, too near to tears to trust her voice.

Furiously, Tony flung her back against the pillows and sprang out of bed.

'I'll fix her!' he said, the effect of the half-bottle of whisky he had consumed since supper making him reel a little as his feet first touched the carpet. He steadied himself and marched over to the door. In an instant Harriet was beside him, clutching his arm.

'Tony, what are you going to do? Leave her, Tony, please. She'll quieten in a moment!'

He pulled her hand from his arm, bruising her fingers as he knocked it against the wall. Then he strode out along the landing and opened the door of the baby's nursery.

His intention was to put the child downstairs where its cries could no longer be heard. He meant it no harm. But his violent temper, together with the effects of the alcohol, made him incautious; as he reached the top of the landing, the carrycot held awkwardly in front of him, his foot slipped. A moment later the cot was upside down at the foot of the stairs, and the baby's cries came to an appalling stop.

Tony stood looking down, shaken into a deadly sobriety by the shock of what had happened. He felt Harriet push past him; saw, as if he were dreaming, the curve of her back as she bent down over the cot; saw her clasp the tiny limp body of his daughter in her arms; heard her say in a voice that might have been announcing the time of day:

'She's dead, Tony. You've killed her.'

Then and then only did he realize what he had done.

*　　　　*　　　　*

'Paul. I want Paul. Please will someone get Paul? Paul . . . Paul!'

Tony listened to his wife's voice, endlessly repeating another man's name, and a little of his old truculence returned. Harriet had been and still was very ill. For the three days prior to the inquest she was perfectly all right, or so Tony imagined. He was agreeably surprised at her behaviour. After that first dreadful accusation she showed no sign of hysteria, shed no tears, in fact seemed far less upset by what had happened than he was. One might have thought she had lost a pet dog rather than her own child—and a child she had made such a fuss about, too.

Fully anticipating her condemnation, Tony had been amazed that she never again turned on him. At the inquest she gave evidence quite calmly, and although her hands trembled there was no expression in her voice. She kept from the judge as she had kept from the doctor the fact that he, Tony, had had too much to drink the night before.

'My husband was taking the baby's cot down to another room. The staircase is very narrow and somehow he tripped. When I got downstairs she was already dead!'

Only Eileen, who was present at Paul's request, could guess from her nursing experience that Harriet was in such a severe state of shock that she was only just aware of what was going on around her; that she had not yet allowed her mind to accept the fact that Antonia was dead; nor that Tony, should the facts become known, could be charged with manslaughter.

It was only by chance that Paul and Eileen knew of the tragedy. It was, of course, reported in the local paper, and because of a lack of any political news the nationals had reprinted the story. There Eileen had happened to glance at it and had rushed to Paul with the news.

'She'll need someone, Eileen. You must go. Can you get away? She must have someone with her.'

Paul had been desperate with anxiety and had told Eileen why he could not be there. Eileen applied for compassionate leave and without asking Harriet's permission arrived at the cottage with her suitcase, saying she had come to stay. It was Tony who told her what had really happened. Still suffering from shock and remorse himself, he admitted to the fact that he'd been drinking and had turned away from Eileen's look of disgust.

'I'll make it up to her, Eileen. When the inquest is over, I'm going to take her back to London. I'll give her a good time and she'll forget all about it in a little while. She can even have another baby if she wants it.'

'If I were your wife, I don't think I'd ever want to see you again,' Eileen said.

Tony bridled at the criticism.

'Well, no one asked you to come here and criticize. Why not go back to London if that's the way you feel?'

'I'm staying,' Eileen had said. 'Unless Harriet asks me to go.'

But Harriet seemed not to care one way or another. She accepted Eileen's presence with the same calm unconcern that she faced the inquest and, later, the drive back to London. Right up to the moment she came upon one of the baby's tiny matinée jackets, left by mistake at the flat, her complete detachment remained, and then, quite suddenly, she broke.

Paul had been right—she needed someone

then. It was Eileen who called the doctor; who arranged for a day and night nurse; who sat with Harriet listening to the sobs that racked her body; who tried to stem the steadily rising temperature with cold spongings and drugs. It was Eileen who was there when, delirious now, Harriet began to call for Paul.

'What's she want him for?' Tony burst out. 'She has a perfectly good doctor of her own.'

Eileen did not mention the reason she believed Harriet wanted Paul, but said briefly:

'It's possible she is re-living the time her baby was born. She doesn't know what she's saying. You can't do any good here, Tony. Why not go out and get drunk?'

'I'll be glad when that other nurse arrives tomorrow!' Tony flung at her furiously. 'You virgins are all the same.'

Eileen stood up and slapped his face. For a moment Tony stood there looking as if he might hit her back, then his eyes dropped and he went quietly enough from the room.

'Paul, Paul . . .' Harriet's voice went on through the night and steadily her temperature rose.

At two in the morning Eileen telephoned the local doctor. Harriet's temperature had risen to 105. The doctor came round immediately and shook his head.

'She ought to be in hospital,' he said. 'I daren't move her now though. Who is she calling for, Nurse? Isn't her husband here?'

149

Briefly Eileen explained who Paul was, giving the same possible reason for Harriet's wish to have him by her side as she had given to Tony.

'Well, if it's possible, I think you'd better get hold of von Murren. Those drugs should have taken the temperature down. Do you know where the doctor is?'

An hour later Paul was at Harriet's bedside and Eileen left them alone. Whatever passed between them now was not her concern, and the look in Paul's eyes told her that he was past caring for anything in the world but the woman he loved.

He sat by Harriet's bed, holding her hand and occasionally wiping the sweat from her forehead. Every time she called for him he told her quietly that he was there and, unconscious though she was, she would remain quiet for a little while. Then, feverishly, she would call his name again.

The hours passed slowly. Paul was not aware of time, not aware of his own tiredness, his whole being concentrated on the determination to get Harriet through this crisis. And slowly but surely the strength of his love, his will, made itself felt in Harriet's tired brain. The fever of her body began to cool and then dropped alarmingly. Paul quickly sent Eileen for more blankets and hot-water bottles. Somewhere, sometime, he was aware that Tony was around, but he shut him out of

Harriet's room without a second glance.

Harriet's teeth began to chatter and her body to shiver. Paul wrapped the blankets more closely round her.

'I'll go and make some tea,' Eileen said. 'I've no doubt there'll be some brandy in the house. That might help.'

As she left the room, Paul saw Harriet's eyelids flicker and then, her eyes enormous and dark with pain, she looked fully at him. Just for that one second he saw happiness dart into them as she recognized him. The effect was as the sun appearing for a brief instant from behind a cloud. Then pain swept across her face again and she whispered:

'Paul, I'll never see my baby again . . . never . . . never . . .'

'Darling, don't think about it—please try not to think about it. It won't always be like this, I promise you. No one can go on grieving to this extent for long; nature doesn't allow it.'

'Paul, I loved her . . . I loved her. I want my baby back!'

'I know, darling, I know. I loved her, too, just as I've always loved you. You know that, don't you?' He tried to distract her thoughts from her child. 'I've always loved you, always, all my life.'

'Paul!' She looked at him with incomprehension. 'You wrote—you said in your letter . . .'

'I know. I had to say something. I dared not

151

let you know how desperately I cared. I've always loved you, Harriet, always.'

'Oh, Paul!' She could not stop the tears that flowed down her cheeks. She could not fully grasp what he was saying to her, far less its implications. All she knew was that when she most needed him he had come to her, loving her as he had always done. He had always been there when she most wanted the comfort of his presence; when she was a young, awkward, lonely girl at her first big party; when she was enduring the agony of bearing her child; when she was suffering the worse agony of losing her.

'Paul, he killed her!' she said, her voice rising hysterically. 'He wanted her out of the way and he killed her.'

He put his arms round her and held her tightly.

'No, Harriet, you know that isn't true. He slipped and fell and it was an accident. It could have happened to anyone.'

'He didn't love her—not as I loved her; not as any normal father would love his child. I'll never forgive him, Paul—never.'

'You say that because hate is a less painful emotion than grief,' Paul told her quietly. 'But you have to forgive him, Harriet. In time you will. When you're quite well again.'

'I don't want to get well. I want to die. I don't want to go on living, Paul.'

'I know that is how you feel,' Paul said. 'But

152

you must not think of yourself, Harriet. Think, if you like, of me. I love you more than anything in this world. If you did not get better, I should wish myself dead, too. You must get well again, Harriet . . . want to get well . . . for my sake if not for your own.'

His need for her, so desperately apparent in his voice, penetrated her mind and touched deep down in her heart. Paul loved her, wanted her to get well for his sake because he loved her, loved her. And the answering echo of her heart admitted her love for him. Never, never could she love Tony again—if she had ever done so! It was only for Paul she wished to go on living, only for Paul, because he would be unhappy if she died.

'For you—' she began, but at that moment the door opened and Eileen came in with a cup of tea.

Paul stood up at once and within a moment was spooning the hot, sweet liquid between Harriet's lips. Drowsiness began to envelop her and yet she struggled against the desire for sleep, knowing there was something she had been about to say to Paul, something she wanted to tell him. But before she could do so her mind slipped away into oblivion and Paul turned to Eileen with a sigh of relief.

'It's all right now, Eileen. She's sleeping. I think she'll pull through all right now, although, poor darling, she's going to be pretty low for a while. She'll need a good long holiday, preferably away from that—'

'You don't have to say it,' Eileen broke in with a grin. 'I think the same about him and I'm not in love with his wife. Paul, what *is* going to happen? Will she stick with him after this? Could any woman go on loving a man who's done what he has done to her?'

'God knows!' Paul said wretchedly. 'Oh, Eileen, if you knew how much at this moment I'm wishing I were anything in the world but a doctor. If I were anything else, I'd take her away and show her how she's wasting her life with that man. But I can't do it . . . and not because I think it's wrong to come between man and wife—though in most cases I do think it wrong—but because I *am* a doctor.'

Eileen drew in her breath.

'I suppose it is rather a muddle!' she said with understatement. 'If you went away with Harriet, Tony could cite you as co-respondent and you might be struck off.'

'Exactly!' Paul said dryly. 'And even if I threw up my career, which I'd do, Eileen, for her happiness, how could we live? I can't ask her to come to a man who hasn't even a job.' He lifted his hands and stared with dislike at them, so useless for any manual work while so gentle and efficient as a doctor. 'I couldn't even get work as a labourer.'

'I expect you could get some kind of work,' Eileen said. 'But, Paul, you couldn't throw up your career. It's not just as if you were an

154

ordinary doctor. They all say you're destined for great things. You've a duty towards the rest of the world. You can't chuck that up just because—'

'Just because I love Harriet and she needs me?' Paul finished wearily. 'If it was only me, I wouldn't hesitate, Eileen, not for an instant. What do you think success means to me beside my love for her? Nothing . . . nothing! Why do you have to remind me that the world needs doctors so badly?'

'Because deep in your heart you know it,' Eileen said calmly. 'You know, better than I do, how desperate they are in your country, in Europe, everywhere, for men like you. It would be years of training thrown away and money, not even your own money, Paul, utterly wasted. It would be destroying so many people's faith in you, trust in you. You cannot and must not consider one woman's happiness against so much. She wouldn't want it, Paul. No woman would. She'd never allow it.'

He knew Eileen was right and that there could be no hope for him or Harriet. Yet his heart struggled to find a loophole—any loophole. And there was none.

'If ever she should ask me—' he began, but Eileen broke in, saying:

'She won't, Paul, and you know she won't. I don't know if she loves you or not, but I do know her well enough to be sure that she'd never let your career suffer, however much she loved or needed you. She's too fine a person. If she knew what this kind of thing did to you she would never subject you to it. When she is well again, she'll remember you love her and she'll be unhappy as well as glad. You mustn't make it more difficult for her, Paul. It'll be hard enough for her to make a life for herself after what's happened without being torn apart by her love for you.'

'I don't know if she does love me,' Paul said miserably. 'Perhaps it is better that way. If I knew it for certain, I don't think I'd have the courage or the will to leave her. She's lost so much, Eileen. Life has been far from easy for her.'

'Life seldom is uncomplicated,' Eileen said with a wisdom beyond her years. 'But it has a way of sorting itself out somehow, Paul. And time is supposed to heal most things. It'll help her to come to terms with the loss of her child, and help you to forget about her.'

'Never!' Paul vowed. 'In eight long years I never stopped loving her. It'll go on for the rest of my life.'

'Perhaps, but not with such intensity,' Eileen said wisely. 'When my mother died, I was only sixteen. I loved her as much as any girl could love her mother. I thought I'd never get over the grief or the loneliness of being without her. I miss her still . . . but I'm able to be happy.'

Paul knew she was right; knew deep down inside that grief, however real, could not be lasting at such intensity. He had seen so much of it, during the war, in the refugee camps . . . women who had lost children, lovers, husbands, children who had lost parents, people nearly insane with the agony of their loss. But they learned to live with it, just as he had learned to live without Harriet once before.

'I'll go now, Eileen,' he said, suddenly determined. 'If she asks for me again, then I must come, no matter what it costs me. But I won't speak of love again to her—won't do anything that might lead to a different relationship between us. As soon as she's well again I'll drop out of her life.'

But it was weeks before Harriet recovered. She seemed to have so little will to get better and only Paul's visits could bring a little colour to her cheeks or a smile to her eyes.

She remembered little of that night when he had spoken again of his love for her. It had become confused in her mind with the dreams she had lived through when the fever was so high and she made no effort to sort reality from delirium.

Had she probed deep enough she would have realized that she was deliberately refraining from facing up to the consequences of Paul's love for her, or of her unadmitted love for him. While she did not think of it, she could accept the friendly, impersonal visits, happy in the quietness of spirit and ease of

157

mind it brought her. For Paul was the only person to whom she could speak of the baby she had lost. To him she could express something of the emptiness of her life, her reluctance to have another child. The only subject they never discussed was Tony. By mutual consent, neither mentioned his name, though he was often there in the flat when Paul called.

Tony was a problem Harriet knew she must face alone. She no longer loved him . . . that fact she accepted without question. She saw him now for what he was and as she despised him, so a certain amount of pity for him replaced the anger at what he had done to their child. And Tony had changed. With her complete disinterest in him, Tony had suddenly begun to need her. By some strange twist of his nature, what he could not have was always the most desirable thing in the world to him. Knowing he had lost Harriet's love piqued him sufficiently to make him want it back, desperately. Her refusal even to speak of the accident, the baby, made his innermost feelings of guilt more real and uncomfortable, and he began to long to hear her say she forgave him. For a while he tried to convince himself that her protection of him at the inquest was because she still cared about him. But he knew now it was not so.

He knew, too, that Harriet derived no pleasure from his presence; knew that there was only one person who could bring a smile of welcome to her eyes—Paul von Murren.

Tony's twisted mind became violent with a jealousy he had never felt before of any human being. Any girl he had ever wanted had been his for the asking and he had taken many in his past away from former boy-friends. He did not in the least care for this new role and was determined somehow or other to end it.

Studying his appearance in his shaving mirror, he was forced to admit that he looked older than his years. Hard living and hard drinking had put lines of dissipation on that otherwise handsome face. He could not see how the full loose line of his mouth betrayed the vain, sensuous, shallow man that lay beneath the virile exterior he presented to the world and to women in particular. That a lot of men did not like him Tony put down to envy. There were plenty whom he called his friends, in reality the hangers-on and spongers after his hospitality and money, who gave him a false sense of popularity.

Tony could not and would not believe that Harriet really preferred von Murren. Good-looking though Paul might be and undoubtedly attractive to women with that fair, Nordic hair and vivid blue eyes, Tony would not accept that he was outclassed in this respect. And because his own values were based for the most part merely on appearances, he did not stop to consider what might be in the other

159

man's character to attract Harriet in a way he never could. So he blamed the accident, telling himself that Harriet had turned against him on that account—the obvious and far more palatable explanation.

Tony waited, wisely, until Harriet was out of bed and convalescent. Then he decided to clear the air once and for all. Purposefully obtuse, he announced one evening:

'Now you're better, Harriet, there won't presumably be any necessity for von Murren to come round so often.'

Harriet looked up from the comfortable armchair in which she lay with her long, slim legs curled beneath her. Her Italian-cut hair had grown during her illness and now lay in childish curls about her shoulders. The immediate effect was of a young girl, but on closer inspection it was apparent to anyone that she was no longer a girl but a woman. There were lines of suffering round her mouth, dark violet shadows about the eyes, and a curiously hard expression in their hazel-green depths.

'Paul doesn't come here as my doctor, Tony. He comes as my friend.'

Her bluntness put him momentarily off-balance. This was not the old Harriet, anxious to justify herself in his eyes, eager to please him, quick to apologize.

'Dash it all, old thing, he comes practically every day of the week!'

160

'That is not true. He comes when he is off duty and that is seldom more than three times a week.'

Tony walked across to the cocktail cabinet and poured himself a drink.

'So early?' he heard Harriet's voice speak critically from behind him. 'It's only just five o'clock.'

'I'll drink when I damn well please.' Tony flared into his quick temper. He never enjoyed criticism, the less so when it was justified.

To further his irritation, Harriet turned back to her book. For a moment he was tempted to walk over and dash the book out of her hand. Her cool imperturbability infuriated him. He would not be ignored.

'It's time we had this out,' he said at last, his voice all but a shout. 'I've had enough of it, Harriet.'

To his incredible surprise, Harriet looked up again from her book and said quietly:

'Well, that makes two of us, Tony. What do you want, a divorce?'

CHAPTER TEN

A few months ago, Tony might have agreed he would be glad to have back his freedom. Not that he had ever really lost his bachelor ways, for he had come and gone as he pleased, Harriet seemingly unquestioning his movements and quite unsuspicious of what he did when he was away from her. All the same, he had had to be careful ever since that time she had discovered he'd been away with a girl and he had sometimes wondered if it was all worth it. He knew now that it was. As a married man, none of his casual girl-friends got to the pitch of expecting him to marry them . . . a clear advantage. Moreover, Harriet's dependence on him had flattered his vanity and he missed it now. He had often thought her incredibly childish and sentimental and been bored by her efforts to please him, the sadistic part of his nature making him wish to hurt her whenever she was most vulnerable.

But, as had happened before, she had only to refuse him admittance to her bed, to become immediately the most desirable woman he knew, and now that she had openly expressed her wish for a divorce, he knew that he would never consent. *She* should not be the one to leave *him*. He, if it ever came to the point, would leave her. No one was going to make him look ridiculous in the eyes of his friends.

There was more to it than that, Tony now realized, looking at Harriet's pale face and set mouth. He wanted her for herself. There was some quality in her which he did not understand and had never stopped to consider until now, that was worth more than any other girl had given him. The others merely played at loving, getting as much as they gave and no more. Harriet had a depth of feeling that those others knew nothing of.

For the first time in his life, Tony was forced to admit to himself that he respected his wife. He might make fun of her deep moral sense: of her sentimentality, of her passionate interest in him and his happiness to the exclusion of her own. But now he could see for himself that she had given him everything and that, fool that he was, he had never valued it until it was all but lost to him.

'No, I don't want a divorce,' he said with a calmness he was far from feeling. 'All I want is that we should put an end to this—this feud that seems to have developed between us.'

'Feud?' Harriet stressed the word. 'Perhaps you mean rift?'

'Call it what you wish,' Tony retorted. 'It's got to stop, Harriet. How much more do you think I can take?'

Harriet laughed, without humour but with a wealth of bitterness in her voice.

'I would have thought it was more a question of how much more I can take,' she said at last. 'And the answer to that is no more, Tony. I'm through, finished!'

Tony moved across the room towards her but let his hands drop to his sides as he saw her shrink away from his touch.

163

'You make it pretty obvious how you feel,' he said bitterly. 'How much longer must I go on paying the price of that wretched accident?'

Harriet's voice rose.

'All your life, Tony . . . just as I shall have to pay the price, too, for as long as I live.'

'You believe I meant to do it?' Tony asked.

Harriet leant back against the chair cushions, her eyes closed against the pain of her thoughts.

'No! I believe it was an accident, Tony, but an accident caused by too much drink. I'll never forgive you for that.'

'Yet you exonerated me from blame at the inquest!' Tony cried. 'Why did you do that if you blamed me?'

'Why? I suppose because I still have some pride left, Tony. I didn't want the world to know what kind of man I'd married.'

'Apparently you hate me!' Tony said angrily.

Harriet drew in her breath.

'No, I don't hate you. I just don't care about you any more one way or another.'

She could not have chosen words more calculated to provoke him, although she had no wish to do so. Her indifference was one thing he could not and would not stand.

'You're my wife, Harriet. You can't say things like that. I can understand you hating me for . . . for the baby's sake, that's only reasonable; but you've got to give me a chance to make up for it. After all, she was my child,

164

too. You don't stop to think what her death meant to me.'

Harriet felt her barrier of defence weaken for the first time. It was true. She had never considered what Antonia's death meant to Tony. She had been so wrapped up in her own appalling agony that she had not wanted to think about anyone else's suffering. Yet it was possible Tony had suffered, and not just from feelings of guilt. He *had* been very proud of the baby, and except for his impatience with her when she cried he had seemed to be glad of her. Yet that wasn't love as she understood the word. Even if Tony had loved the baby it would not make any difference to her feelings for him.

The baby's death had done more than shock her mind. It had given her, for the first time in her life, a completely new side to her nature. She saw things without sentiment for what they were. She saw Tony without the eyes of love and therefore recognized him for the first time for what he was . . . a good-looking, self-centred, pleasure-loving young man without a grain of responsibility in him; without depth or emotions beyond the call of his bodily needs. She saw him as a useless parasite living on the money his parents had left him, wasting his life and hers.

'I'm sorry, Tony. I just don't love you any more. I can never love you again. It hasn't really anything to do with . . . with Antonia's death.' Strange how she could speak about it at last!

'Then it's because of von Murren!' Tony burst out. 'I've been too damned trusting about you two. All the time he's been making love to you.'

'Tony!' Her voice cut across the room almost like a slap in the face. Her face was deathly pale and the hands she clasped together were trembling despite their grip. 'That's a lie, and you know it. I don't deny he loves me. He's loved me ever since we were little more than children. I don't deny I love him. But he has only once spoken of it and he doesn't know I'm in love with him. He's never made love to me . . . or spoken of his love for me except on that one occasion.'

'So you don't deny you're in love with him?'

'No! I don't deny it. I'm not even sorry about it, Tony. I should have married him all those years ago. We understand each other in a way you and I have never done.'

'Then why did you marry me?' Tony shouted at her, infuriated by her calm voice and her outspoken rejection of him.

'Because I believed myself in love with you, Tony. I'd have gone to the other end of the world for you. Your happiness was all that mattered to me.'

'Well, what's changed you, if it isn't von Murren? You say it has nothing to do with the baby, that you *were* in love with me. All right,

166

so it must be because of von Murren.'

'No!' Harriet drew in her breath as she searched for the truth. 'No, it was only after I'd stopped loving you that I knew I was in love with Paul. Perhaps it *was* to do with Antonia's death; that's when I first started to see you without the rose-coloured spectacles, Tony. I fought against it and tried not to see you without the eyes of love. I didn't want our marriage to break up, not even when you . . . when the baby died. Unfortunately I couldn't make myself feel anything for you any more. I have only suddenly realized I still love Paul. That's why I wanted him near me when my life seemed useless and hopeless; when I wanted to die. You see, I discovered that his friendship meant more to me than your love had ever done.'

'You're enjoying this, aren't you, Harriet? You know how much you're hurting me and you're getting your own back now for the times I've hurt you. All right, I can understand that, but here's something for you to understand. Von Murren isn't going to have you. *You're my wife*, do you hear? If you try to leave me for him, I'll blast his name across every front page of every paper in the country. *Doctor cited as co-respondent.*'

'Stop it, Tony!' She was standing up now, her eyes blazing, a spot of vivid red standing out on her high cheekbones. 'You can't touch Paul, do you hear me? You haven't a single

167

shred of evidence against him.'

'Oh, no, not *evidence*,' Tony said with deadly sarcasm. 'But how many doctors do you think would survive so much publicity? He'd get off all right, but the damage would be done by then—and you'd still be legally tied to me. You don't think I'm going to sit back and give you evidence for a divorce, do you?'

Divorce had not entered Harriet's mind until this evening, nor had she considered that she and Paul could ever hope to be together. Her love for Paul had come to her quietly and almost unnoticed, not as a startling revelation. She hadn't even allowed herself to think about it but had just accepted the knowledge and been happy in it, happy in the same quiet way as when he visited her. Her state of mind and health had forbidden her searching for reasons, for action, for hope. She had lived entirely for the present.

But now Tony had forced her into the open, forced her to see what really had happened to her and to Paul. Paul loved her and she loved him and she was Tony's wife.

With sudden insight she said:

'You don't really want me, Tony; you never have wanted a wife—only a mistress. You're saying all this because your vanity is hurt. You don't want any other man to have me.'

'You're damned right I don't,' Tony replied with violence. 'What's more, no man is going to take my wife away from me. I've warned you

168

what will happen if you go on seeing him. I'll sue you for divorce and implicate him as far as I'm able. He'll end up hating you, for it will surely ruin his so-promising career! He wouldn't get off so lightly, my dear Harriet, coming here at all hours of the day and night, pretending to be interested in your health and really only wanting your body—'

His words came to an abrupt halt as Harriet's hand stung with all the force she could muster against his cheek. For a moment, surprise held him still, then with a laugh he caught her by the shoulders and looked down into her white, furious face.

'You know, my dear, you surprise me. I often thought you were a bit tame. It seems there are fires hidden beneath that cool exterior of yours. I always did find you most attractive when that reserve went and I like a woman with spirit. I can see I've been treating you quite the wrong way.'

She looked up into his sneering face, wishing she had the strength to break away from his grasp. She hated him now—really hated him. Her one thought became centred in the desire to get away from him and never to have to see him again.

'Let me go. You're hurting me.'

'Oh, no, my dear, I shan't let you go. I'm not such a fool. If you walk out of this house, I'll smear von Murren with all the mud I can rake up. Is that what you want?'

'You couldn't . . . you wouldn't, Tony . . .' But she had only to look into his eyes to know that he would. The strength went from her body and as he released his hold on her she fell back on to the chair, covering her face with her hands.

'I'll find some way to leave you,' she whispered. 'Your life hasn't been blameless, Tony. What about that girl you took on that sailing weekend?'

'Don't be a silly little fool!' Tony said with a laugh as he walked away from her to pour himself another whisky. He felt quite in command of the conversation now. 'You condoned that offence months ago, remember? Besides, I'd defend the case and counter-sue you and cite your precious Paul.'

I can't stand any more of this, Harriet thought. Even Tony couldn't be so despicable. She had once thought she loved him . . . she *had* loved him. He couldn't really be like this, not Tony, the father of her child.

'I'm going to bed,' she said at last. 'I'm locking my door, Tony, and not even your threats will make me unlock it, so don't try.'

With some dignity she left the room, Tony smiling after her enigmatically.

He was beginning to feel some shame at what he had said. He wasn't really evil. He'd never done anyone any harm in his life, not intentionally. It wasn't his fault if sometimes things went wrong and someone did get hurt.

The baby, for instance . . .

He poured himself another drink and made it stiffer this time. He'd reached the maudlin stage and badly needed cheering up. Resentment at his misfortune replaced the momentary remorse. Harriet was his wife, and he'd given her everything. She'd no right to treat him like this. Let her suffer for it—let von Murren suffer for it, too. He was the one who was really to blame. Well, he'd see they didn't meet again. He'd nip that affair in the bud. In time Harriet would forget him and that would be that.

Such was Tony's conceit that he really believed he could make Harriet fall in love with him again. He didn't even add that he might need luck. As her mother had done once before, he thought it needed only time and distance to separate her from Paul for good and all.

*　　　*　　　*

Harriet sat beside Paul in his car and stared down over the valley below Reigate Hill. From here, on this clear spring morning with a threat of rain in the sky, it was possible to see the South Downs. She would have liked to go there; to walk with Paul across the top of the downs; to hear the larks sing and perhaps see a hare dart through the stiff grass.

'Now tell me, Harriet, what has happened?

171

You sounded desperate on the phone this morning. I shouldn't really be here but I had to come.'

Paul's voice was anxious, bewildered, but softened as always by his great love for her.

'Paul, I couldn't ask you to come to the mews. Not after what happened. I shouldn't really be here, either. It's too dangerous.'

Paul's blue eyes widened.

'Dangerous? Harriet, you must tell me what all this is about. Start at the beginning.'

She twisted her hands together in her lap. What she had to say was so horrible, she knew it would take all her courage to bear out her intention. She loved Paul and he loved her, yet she had come to tell him they mustn't see each other again—*ever.* Nothing must harm Paul or his career. Nothing! Moreover, she could not even tell him of her love for him. That would only make it harder for him.

'It's Tony!' she said, choosing her words carefully. 'It seems he's become terribly jealous of you, Paul. He—he thinks you're in love with me and—'

'Well, he's right there,' Paul broke in. 'We both know that, so why not let us speak of it, Harriet? There's nothing for you to be afraid of or upset about. I've known ever since we met again that you were beyond my reach, and I've accepted it.'

She turned to face him, her eyes desperate as she pleaded with him.

172

'Paul, *please*! This only makes it more difficult for me.'

He resisted the temptation to take her in his arms. Denying himself the right to touch her had become second nature to him now and he had all but perfected his self-control.

'All right, Harriet. Go on!'

'He thinks . . . thinks I'm in love with you, too.' She ignored his indrawn breath and quickly looked away from him lest he should see the truth in her eyes. 'He has told me that if I try to leave him, or even see you again, he's going to sue me for divorce and cite you as co-respondent.'

'But that's ridiculous!' Paul burst out. 'We've never done anything wrong—'

'Oh, Paul, I know, I know!' she broke in, her fingers twisting her gloves in her nervousness. 'But he knows what kind of publicity such a case would get. It isn't that he wants a divorce . . . he doesn't. He just wants to hurt you.'

'But why?' Paul asked, stunned by this new aspect of Tony. 'He can't really believe you love me. You've never given him any reason to think so, have you?'

Harriet bit her lip. How she hated the necessity of lying to Paul of all people! How she longed with her whole heart to admit the truth to him!

'I suppose I openly prefer your company to his,' she said at last with a trace of bitterness. 'It was you I called for when I had that

173

breakdown. And I've always been so pleased to see you when you've come to visit me . . .'

'But that's not enough,' Paul said violently. 'He must have guessed that you didn't feel much like *his* company after what happened. It was only to be expected. But you are his wife, Harriet. He knows he can trust you.'

'He knows I don't love him any more,' Harriet said, her inner revulsion clear enough in her tone of voice. 'I'm sorry if this seems disloyal to my husband, but I have to tell you to make you understand. We have to say good-bye, Paul, for always. Otherwise he'll find some way to hurt you.'

Paul had always known he must lose her sooner or later. He had promised his own mother that he would go out of her life. Now Harriet was telling him the same thing. It was the right thing to do, he knew that, and he was not arguing about it. But there were some things he still had to know. What was going to happen to Harriet now? If she really wasn't in love with Tony any longer, would she go on living with him? What kind of life would it be, for Tony or for her? Yet she said he had threatened to sue her for divorce if she left him. They must have spoken of separating.

'You must tell me, Harriet. What put all this into his mind? Did you tell him you wanted to leave him?'

'I don't know . . . yes I did, Paul. I don't want to go on living with him now. But for a

174

time, anyway, there's no alternative. He can do us such harm.'

Paul squared his shoulders.

'That's absurd. We are both innocent. It's no crime that I love you. Except for that admission, I've done nothing to be ashamed of. Let him do his worst, Harriet.'

She turned back to him, placing her hand on his arm, unconscious of the effect her touch had on him. She was concerned only in making him understand the danger.

'Paul, you've got to see it not the way it has been, but as Tony could present it. You've come to my bedroom, you've sat with me into the early hours of the morning when I was so ill—'

'Yes, but I was there as a doctor,' Paul said stupidly.

'Exactly, Paul! You've been both as a doctor and as a friend. Oh, I've lain awake all last night imagining all the awful stories that could be made up about us. Don't you see, Paul? It's about the worst thing that could happen to you. You could be struck off the register, even though you're innocent. There's only our word for it that nothing passed between us. You don't even deny you love me.'

For the first time, Paul realized the seriousness of the situation. He saw exactly what might happen. He'd read such stories before now and the less reputable newspapers made the most of them. But against that fear

175

for his reputation, his career, was the fear for Harriet's future. He would not have her sacrificing herself for him.

'But, Harriet, it means you'll have to go on living with him if he really intends to go through with his threat. Surely he can't mean it. He must have spoken in the heat of the moment.'

Harriet had considered that, too. Tony might not have meant it, but she dared not take the chance. She would stop seeing Paul and she would stay with Tony. Perhaps in time he would forget Paul and give her her freedom. Without Paul to go to, her freedom meant little enough to her. She merely baulked at the idea of living a lie with Tony, for she could never again be a real wife to him. He must know that. She would stay with him but she would be his wife in name only. Even he could not try to force his attentions on her.

For a moment her courage failed her. Last night Tony had taken her in his arms and told her he still found her attractive—more so when she was angry. Suppose he did try to make love to her . . .

She looked up and met Paul's eyes. The blue seemed darkened now almost to black, the dark sweep of lashes oddly in contrast with the fair hair. She knew that she had never loved him more than she did at this moment. Nor had he ever seemed so attractive. He looked so young and strong and clean and yet completely masculine with his long straight nose, the firm jaw and wide, generous, sensitive mouth.

Paul, Paul! her heart cried to him.

'You've no need to worry about me,' she said, turning away from him yet again so that he should not see she lied to him. 'I've no objection to living with him so long as he leaves me alone. I think maybe I'll go away for a while, for a holiday. I think he'll let me go if he realizes we shan't be meeting any more and if I give him my word I'll come back to him. Hc knows I've never lied to him and that he can trust me. Once I've had a rest it won't seem so bad.'

'If I could only take you away for good!' The words were wrung from him before he could prevent them. 'If you'd only let him divorce you, Harriet, and let me marry you. I know you aren't in love with me, but I could make you happy. I'm sure I could.'

Her whole being trembled now. She tried to keep her emotions under control.

'It's no good, Paul. You'd lose your job and you'd never get over that . . . nor should I for having been the cause of it. You've got to forget about me, Paul, for my sake as much as for your own.'

Paul looked at the bent, dark head, the soft white curve of her neck, the long slim line of her back. Forget her . . . how impossible it would be! He knew every line of her face; the

177

smooth forehead, the high cheekbones, the slightly tilted nose, the sweet curve of her lips. How could he forget them ever? He knew her every expression, too. He had seen her face in repose, in pain, in suffering, in happiness. He knew every intonation of her voice. And he loved her.

For the second time in his life, Paul hated his chosen profession. Had he been anything else but a doctor he could have withstood the unpleasantness of a divorce. Many in the world might condemn him, but when the husband was such a man as Tony, the wife such as Harriet, good and trusting and without evil in her, she must surely be forgiven for leaving him.

If he'd known she loved him, Paul would have thrown up his career in order to make her happy. But even as he realized it was within the realms of possibility that she might come to love him in time, he knew also that he had no right to suggest it. If she could in fact tolerate the thought of continuing a life with Tony, it was not for him to stand between them.

'Harriet! Where will you go? I shall worry about you desperately!'

'I'll think of somewhere,' Harriet said with an attempted smile. 'Europe, probably.'

'Harriet, would you go to the Tyrol? To my home? My mother could look after you and help you to get well and strong again.' His voice warmed to the thought and he became filled with determination to make her go there. 'It's very beautiful there, especially at this time of the year, and there would be sunshine now, too. Harriet, would you?'

Harriet felt her hcart beating so that it almost suffocated her. To see Paul's home . . . meet his mother . . . live where *he* had lived as a small boy. It would be pleasure and pain too. He could not know how much she would suffer at being so near to him and yet so completely out of his life. If Tony would let her go, she would do so. It would make Paul happy to think of her there, and she might find rest and a certain peace in the mountains.

'I'll talk to Tony. He—he might be against the idea,' she said hesitantly. 'But if he knows you won't be there he might agree. I'd love to go, Paul.'

'I'll write to my mother tonight, telling her to get in touch with you,' Paul said eagerly. 'You'll be so happy there, Harriet. There'll be snow on the high slopes, and in the valley all the spring flowers will be out. It's one of the best times of the year. And you'll love my mother . . . no one could help loving her. She'll look after you.'

There were tears now in Harriet's eyes, tears she blinked away before he could see them. This was Paul's first request to her—the only one he had ever made. If it would make him happy for her to go, she would do

179

everything in her power to get there. Yet she knew she could not hope to find happiness. There could never be any happiness anywhere in the world without Paul.

'I . . . I think we ought to go back,' she said suddenly, afraid of her own emotions. 'Tony went out to lunch at the club but he'll be back home at three. He might start asking questions if I'm not there.'

All the fire and enthusiasm had left Paul's voice as he said:

'Then this . . . this is good-bye, Harriet?'

She nodded her head, unable to trust her voice.

He wanted to take her in his arms, to cry out his love for her, his need of her, his utter despair at losing her, but even as he turned and half moved towards her, she said:

'No, don't, Paul! It's more than I can bear. Please, please don't touch me.'

His hands fell to his sides. Naturally she, too, was upset at this parting. She had loved him once and was very fond of him now, depended on him as a friend. He would have been deeply hurt and surprised if she had shown no sorrow at this parting.

If he had touched her at that moment, she would have weakened. No power on earth could have prevented her declaring her love for him. Inside, her whole being was torn apart at the terrible thought of never seeing him again. She dared not look at him, dared not speak. On the long drive back through the traffic into London she sat in silence, biting back the agonizing tears, rigidly keeping herself under control.

She knew she could not face the last words of good-bye that must surely take place when he dropped her off at the flat. Cowardly though it might be, she felt unable to stand any more. Seeing an Underground station a little in front of the car, she said suddenly:

'I'd like some cigarettes, Paul. Could you pull up here?'

'I'll get them for you,' Paul said. But she opened the car door and was out on the pavement before he had moved.

'You mustn't park here,' she said breathlessly. 'Don't wait for me, Paul. Good-bye!'

He sat in stunned silence, seeing her slim, upright figure disappear into the crowds at the mouth of the Underground, oblivious to the angry, impatient hooting of the cars lining up behind him.

She had gone . . . gone . . . quickly and quietly. He would never see her again.

At last Paul was forced to move forward. He let out the clutch and slipped into gear, driving automatically and without thought. Instinct guided him back to the hospital, helped him park the car in its usual spot, and got him to his own room. But though his eyes stared out of the window into the teeming masses struggling below him along the rain-wet streets, he saw only Harriet, hurrying, hurrying as she ran out of his life for ever.

CHAPTER ELEVEN

It was three weeks before Harriet went to Austria . . . three weeks in which she saw a new Tony, a Tony she had not believed could ever exist.

On her return home to the mews she found him waiting for her.

'I wondered where you were. I've been so worried!'

He jumped to his feet and was helping her off with her coat. If she shrank from any physical contact with him he appeared not to notice it. He pulled forward the armchair so that she could warm herself by the fire.

'You're shivering, Harriet. You haven't caught cold? Where have you been?'

'I was saying good-bye to Paul,' she said, her voice toneless, her eyes on the leaping flames. 'We won't be seeing each other any more.'

There was a moment of silence while Tony studied his wife. He did not doubt that she spoke the truth. He was only surprised that she showed so little sign of emotion.

'You really mean that, don't you, Harriet? I can trust you, can't I?'

'I've never lied to you, Tony.'

He gave an embarrassed little cough. He had so often lied to her—small white lies that he excused by telling himself they were to save her feelings.

'Look here, Harriet, I want to apologize for the way I behaved yesterday evening. I was insanely jealous and I didn't know what I was saying. You do understand?'

He had her attention now. The luminous green eyes were staring at him in amazement. For Tony to apologize was one thing, but that he should be explaining his horrible threats was even more unbelievable.

'Really, Harriet, you must see my point of view. No man likes to see his wife being taken away by another man, and right under his nose, too. I trusted you both implicitly because you'd told me when you first saw the fellow again that the affair had died a natural death years ago. It wasn't very fair of you, Harriet, or of him.'

Harriet tried to think coherently. This softly spoken, reasonable Tony was so different from the man she had expected to come back to. Put his way, it did seem as if she and Paul had been playing a game at his expense. Only it wasn't a game.

'He still doesn't know I love him,' she said briefly, nervously. 'There was never any question of his making love to me. We were just friends, Tony.'

'There is no such thing as a platonic friendship between a man and a woman,' Tony argued pointedly. 'If I'd had any sense, I'd have realized that in leaving you alone so much with him I was asking for something more to develop. But there was a reason I did so, Harriet. I knew you couldn't stand the sight of me after . . . after Antonia's death. I felt it wasn't fair to inflict my attentions on you when I only served to remind you of the tragedy. *It was out of consideration for you, Harriet.* Otherwise you might have found me just as understanding, just as attentive as von Murren. You never gave me a chance.'

Is it true? Harriet wondered, trying to sort out these new ideas and link them with the man she had come to believe Tony really was. Had it been her fault that their marriage had come to this near-breaking point? She had hurt him deeply because she had felt she could not look at him without horror. The baby's death had been an accident, albeit caused because Tony had had too much to drink, but had that been her fault, too? Few men could bear for long a fretful crying child without loss of patience. Perhaps she had expected too much of him, more than any ordinary man could give, unless he were like Paul.

'I . . . I did blame you for that accident,' she said at last, speaking slowly and with difficulty, wanting to be fair to him in what she said now. 'Perhaps it was wrong of me to do so. If so, I'm sorry, Tony.'

He leant forward in his chair eagerly.

'Don't you think I'm sorry, too, Harriet? Can't you imagine what it has been like for me, knowing it was my fault, hating myself, knowing you hated me? After all, she was my child too.'

He was very persuasive, very convincing, and Harriet felt herself weaken. This boyish, unhappy Tony was so very different from the pleasure-loving, selfish man she had come to believe she had married. It was almost as if their roles were reversed and instead of her pleading with him for understanding and sympathy he was now pleading with her. Her naturally generous spirit wanted to think the best of him and yet her instinct still fought against it.

'I know you've suffered terribly, Harriet. But so have I. And as if losing the baby wasn't enough, I've lost you, too. You told me last night you didn't love me any more and that you wanted to leave me. It was the last straw, and I felt desperate. I couldn't believe you really meant to desert me.'

'Tony, don't!'

She didn't want to feel sorry for him, yet, despite everything, that was how she was beginning to feel. He was showing her his side of the picture, a side she had never for one instant stopped to consider. She had never imagined that when he went out drinking with

185

his friends he might have been seeking the same friendship, sympathy and solace that she had been looking for from Paul.

'You must forgive me, Harriet, you *must*. I just can't stand this rift between us any longer!'

But she was not yet ready to forgive him. The death of her baby still stood between them, as solid a barrier as her love for Paul, hopeless though it might be.

Her silence was his answer and, realizing it, he tried again to weaken her defences.

'Surely you know I'd do anything in the world for you, Harriet? Anything to make you happy again. Anything to make you care for me again. We'll go away, start life together somewhere else . . . America, if you like. But give me the chance to win you back, *please*, Harriet.'

Harriet stared at him, trying to see the man in front of her in his true light. What was the real Tony? Did he really need her, love her? Was the flippancy only on the surface? Which was the real man beneath that handsome, boyish outward appearance? Had she ever really known him, understood the man she had married? Why couldn't she still love him? What had gone out of her heart when Antonia had died?

'Tony,' she began hesitantly, 'don't you think *you* might be happier without *me*? I never seem to have been very successful as the wife you wanted. We don't have the same interests. You like a very social life and the bright lights. I like country life and books and music. We don't even share the same taste in people. I can see now how tiresome you must have found me; often a spoil-sport and never fully able to fall in with your wishes with my whole heart. Wouldn't you be happier with . . . well, with someone else?'

She was voicing a thought which had often crossed Tony's mind, but which he now denied vigorously. Even if it were true that they were opposite in many ways, there had never been another woman who attracted him as Harriet had done . . . still could do. He sensed the worth of her love, her respect; knew the depth of her passionate nature; knew that she was generous, unselfish and basically good. She had given him a pretty free rein, too. Another woman might have been far more possessive.

'I'd never marry again, never,' he said with the conviction of truth. 'If you leave me, Harriet, I'll go to the dogs.'

No, no, no! whispered a voice inside her. Don't listen to him. Stay free of him. There was never any happiness in loving him.

Yet he was her husband, the man she had vowed to go on loving till she died. She could not keep faith with that vow, much as it had meant to her on her wedding day. She could not love him. But she could stay with him, as long as he needed her, if their marriage still had some meaning for him.

187

'I want to go away for a while by myself,' she said awkwardly. 'I want to get right away from everything, Tony. Paul suggested I should stay with his mother in the Tyrol where there'll be some sunshine and some peace. I'd like to go. If you'll let me, then I'll try to make a fresh start to our married life when I get back.'

It was Tony's turn to hesitate. He didn't enjoy being kept on a hook, but at the same time he realized he might lose her altogether if he were not extremely careful. He dared not rush her. But von Murren's home . . .

'Can't you go somewhere else? You can hardly expect me to like the thought of you being there!'

'Paul will be in London,' Harriet said, wondering how it was she could speak his name so calmly, so evenly. 'I would like to go there, Tony. Hotel life isn't what I need.'

'Why not let me take you away? We might cruise somewhere—I could hire a yacht. We could go round the South Sea Islands. Couldn't we go together, Harriet?'

'No!' Her reply was more abrupt than she had intended, but was wrung from her heart. She didn't want Tony with her, least of all on a romantic journey such as he suggested. She saw his expression and tried to soften the statement. 'I want to be quite alone, Tony, to think things out and to get really well again. Afterwards—'

'All right!' he said. 'We'll go afterwards—

188

just the two of us. It will be like a second honeymoon. You do really mean it, don't you, Harriet? This isn't just a trick to run off with Paul? I can trust you?'

'I promise I'll come back!' Harriet said, little knowing how difficult that promise might be for her to keep. And for the moment Tony was satisfied with this victory, and let her be.

*   *   *

Victoria Station had receded into the distance behind her and Harriet knew that at last she was really on her way. The last few days had been filled with packing and preparations for her journey, with arrangements for Mrs Wood to come in and cook for Tony, as usually happened when she was in the country staying at Henry VIII.

Harriet took out the bundle of tickets, passport, reservation cards that filled her travelling bag, seeing again the imposing list of places through which she must pass on her way to Kitzbühel, one of the large towns of the Tyrol. She had preferred to come by boat and train rather than by air, for she wanted to get to know Paul's country, to which she had never been. He had so often talked of Austria and his home in those years long ago when they had first met. Now, after all this time, she was actually going to see it with her own eyes. If only Paul could have been here in the train

189

beside her, sharing her excitement and delight!

At ten-forty they would be in Dover, and, by half past six this evening, in Brussels. She had a sleeper booked to take her the next stage of the journey, through Aachen, Cologne, Ulm. She found herself sharing the sleeper with a young American girl with whom she quickly struck up a friendship. The girl was pretty, amusing and talkative. Harriet found herself thinking how Tony would have liked her.

Suzanne Perry was on her way to Brixen im Thale, in the Tyrol, for one of the International Courses.

'They sure are fun,' Suzanne told her with enthusiasm. 'I come every year now and I'm never bored.'

'But what do you do?' Harriet asked curiously.

The girl smiled.

'Well, honey, the main idea is a kind of get-together for people of your country and the Austrians, but they didn't raise any objection to an American taking part. To find out about each other's way of life. You get a fine holiday thrown in because you don't have to attend classes unless you want, though you don't get a certificate if you aren't there regularly. There's a language course and a music course. It's the music I'm most interested in, though I take the language course as well. I'm on Advanced German right now. Then we do Austrian Literature, History and Geography, Social

190

Conditions, Art . . . When I go home to the States I'm gonna lecture to the Women's Club. Mom is secretary and she sure was pleased when I gave some talks last summer.'

'I think you're very enterprising,' Harriet said admiringly. She had met before young Americans who seemed far more interested than her own countrywomen in the ways and social conditions of other countries. And many of them seemed to have this girl's keen desire to go on learning even though they had left school.

'Of course, the music is what I really come for. There's the history of music in Austria and the lives of the composers to study, folk-lore and, of course, folk dancing and singing. Never a dull moment, in fact. They take you on coach excursions to Kitzbühel and to the lakes round about. It sure is pretty there.'

'I'm on my way there now,' Harriet said. 'But not to stay. I'm going much higher up to stay with some friends who live in the mountains in a *Schloss*. The "Wild Emperor Mountains" they're called.'

'Gee, honey, those castles are beautiful. I went over the Castle Neuschwanstein in Bavaria on my way home last year. It's like something out of a fairy-story. It was built on a great piece of rock jutting out of the hillside. No one lives there now though. I sure envy you going to live in a real *Schloss*.'

'It is exciting,' Harriet agreed, 'though I

191

believe most of it is shut up now and the owners just have a suite of rooms for their use. Tell me more about Austria.'

'It's just all so pretty I don't know where to begin,' the girl sighed; 'all the pine forests and meadows and lakes. Then there's those lovely little mountain streams, all crystal-clear water because, of course, it's just melted snow from higher up, and waterfalls bubbling down over the rocks . . . sure is pretty.'

'It sounds it,' Harriet said. 'You often go out walking?'

'You bet! I like mountain climbing and skiing too. And I love going into the little guesthouses. They are rather like your English inns only warmer! Everywhere you go there is music and dancing, even in the cafés. And the people are all so friendly. You'd never imagine they'd been through so much in the war.'

'I think the Austrians are just naturally happy,' Harriet agreed. 'All the same, many of them did suffer in the war—my friends did, anyway. The tourist probably doesn't see beneath the surface. You know, there are still thousands of refugees in Austria.'

She told the American girl of Paul's plans to turn the *Schloss* into a clinic. The girl was immediately interested.

'See here, Harriet, if you give me this doctor friend's name and address, I'll try to raise some money for him when I go back home. That's the kind of thing our folks are always

192

willing to help with if they can, and they'd far rather contribute to something like this than to a vast organization. Maybe our town could kind of adopt this idea and send parcels and such. Do you think your doctor would accept?'

'I'm sure he would!' Harriet cried. 'It's wonderfully kind of you. Of course, it may be some years before the idea is put into practice. There is a very large sum of money required, you know. But Paul would gladly send you all the details and be most grateful for any help.'

'I come from a small town called Woodhaven near Pebody in Massachusetts. Maybe they could call one of the wards Woodhaven. It sure would be a thrill for my folk and I can make this the basis for my talks next summer.'

For a while both girls discussed the idea and then eventually went to steep. In the morning they woke to find the train halted for fifteen minutes at Lindau. They breakfasted together in the dining car, passing through Bludens, Langen Arlberg, St Anton and Landeck and Imst before lunch. By half past one they were in Innsbruck and on the last lap of the journey to Kitzbühel, which they reached soon after three.

It was already nearly dark and the town was bright with twinkling lights from the street cafés and houses. One of the biggest resorts in Austria, it was a beautiful picturesque Tyrolean town in magnificent surroundings.

The Schwarsee Lake was nearby for bathing in the summer and boating. And five and six thousand feet above the town towered the snow-covered mountains.

The two girls found they had an hour to spare before their trains took them off in different directions, so they had hot chocolate and wonderful Austrian pastries in a nearby café. They were served by a smiling Austrian girl in peasant costume who spoke nearly perfect English.

She stayed to talk with them for a few moments and enquired their destination. She knew Piller Lake and had seen Paul's home which had been built on its shores.

'It is most beautiful there, *Fräulein*. And now at this time of year it is specially so, for the spring flowers are out and the lake is very blue.'

Saying good-bye to her American friend, Harriet returned to the station to take the smaller local train to Piller. From there she took the old village taxi and was soon being driven up the bumpy stone-covered track that served as a road to the *Schloss*.

It was not until she woke next morning that she saw its full beauty. It was pure medieval architecture with four large turrets reaching up to the incredible blue of the sky, the pinnacled tops like pointing fingers. The rooms were vast and Harriet was able to imagine how imposing they must have been when furnished, for even

194

without the tapestries and carpets to give them warmth and colour the feeling of spacious grandeur was all about her.

Only a suite of rooms on the ground floor had been kept for the *Gräfin* to live in. These were warm and comfortable, though somewhat large as were most of the rooms Harriet could see. There was no doubting the fact that the whole castle could be turned into a perfect convalescent home, though she could see now why Paul said so much money was needed to equip such a vast place, and to supply heat and plumbing and modern comforts.

Harriet only glimpsed the smallest part of the vast interior of the *Schloss* as the old maid, Maria, took her to her room to wash and change before going to meet Paul's mother. Unlike the smiling girl in the café in Kitzbühel, the old peasant greeted her with suspicion and an unhappy look which Harriet found difficult to explain, for Paul had spoken of her as being a faithful, loyal and affectionate old woman, once his nurse.

She was soon to discover the reason, however, for as she went along the stone passage and opened the door of the room Maria had indicated earlier, she was to find Paul's mother lying against a mound of pillows in a vast and beautifully carved four-poster bed.

Harriet stared at the white-haired woman in the bed and her eyes widened in surprise. The

195

Gräfin bore no resemblance to the beautiful, upright, commanding figure Paul had so often described. One side of her face seemed twisted as if she were in pain. Harriet was unable to disguise her confusion.

'Countess von Murren!' she said, going slowly towards the bed. 'I am Harriet . . . Harriet Harley. I hope . . . that is, I trust you are not ill?'

The eyes—Paul's blue eyes, Harriet thought with a jolt—stared up at her with a twisted smile.

'I am afraid I am confined permanently to my bed, my dear.' The voice was weak but still commanding of attention.

'But Paul never said . . .'

'Paul doesn't know. Nor will you tell him. I will let him know when the time comes.'

The accent was nearly faultless but, as with Paul's voice, the foreign intonation still came through.

Impulsively Harriet went towards the bed and touched the hand outstretched to her, then gathered it in her own warm ones.

'Please, *Madame*, you must tell him if you are not well. He would be so distressed; he'd want to come to you.'

The blue eyes smiled.

'Exactly! I do not wish him to be distressed. You see, my dear, there is nothing he can do— nothing any doctor can do. I have had two strokes, the last one leaving me paralysed on my left side. I am afraid that the next one will probably be fatal. Paul, being a doctor, would know this and because he is my son he would not accept it. It would be a needless pain for him to see me die.'

Harriet stared aghast as she realized what she had heard. This was Paul's mother, the woman he adored, with only a short while perhaps to live, and yet Paul did not know it.

'He'd want to be with you, I'm sure he would,' she said desperately. 'There might be something he could do . . .'

'There's nothing that can be done for me. I have seen the best heart specialist in the country. No, my time has come, child, and I am not afraid. Only for Paul. I wish to spare him.'

Harriet looked at the face again, seeing now how beautiful this woman must have been. She tried to control her shocked thoughts.

Here was true unselfishness, she realized, true love that denied its own need for another's happiness. *But Paul would want to be here.* Again she expressed her belief, but again Paul's mother shook her head.

'It would distress him terribly to see me like this,' she said proudly. 'And there is nothing he could do but stay here to await the end. Put yourself in Paul's place. Would you be happy seeing someone you love, knowing they were living from day to day?'

Harriet's mind and imagination saw all too

197

clearly Paul lying here half paralysed awaiting death and her heart recoiled from the thought. She couldn't bear to see him so . . .

'There!' the quiet voice beside her read her thoughts. 'Now let us forget me and talk of other things. You do not look well, my child; you are so thin! I will tell Maria she is to feed you up. When you taste her *apfelstrüdel* you will regain your appetite. Our mountain air is good, too, for it will make you want to eat and it will put colour back in your cheeks. All the same, Paul is quite right when he says you are beautiful.'

The colour flamed into Harriet's cheeks and away again, leaving her heart beating feverishly.

'It is so good of you to have me to stay. Paul was anxious for me to come and said you would be glad to see me. Of course he did not realize you were ill. I will, of course, go home as soon as I can arrange it.'

The *Gräfin* looked directly into Harriet's eyes.

'It would be my great pleasure if you would stay—that is if you can bear with an invalid. I would be much comforted by your company.'

'Of course I'll stay if you really want me to,' Harriet said with sincerity. 'All the same, I cannot understand how you can be so welcoming to me of all people.'

The blue eyes studied the girl.

'I see what it is you are trying to say. You

198

mean because you have not been able to make my son happy? It is true I have sometimes wished he had never met you. But I am older than you, my dear, and life has taught me many things. Love, no matter whether it be returned or not, is always a good thing. Loving you has done much for Paul. It has helped to make a man of him and it has helped him to understand human nature; to be gentle and sympathetic and kind. There was a time during the war when he seemed to derive his greatest pleasure from hate; first hate of the Germans and then hate of the Russians. He was intolerant and even hard. Now he is very different.'

'He is going to be so hurt . . . again!' Harriet cried, appalled by her own thoughts. 'When you . . . when you leave him he will have no one.'

The old lady sighed.

'I know, I know,' she agreed. 'Yet he will have the compensation of his work. It has helped him once before to get over the loss of a loved one—you, my dear—when you were both separated through no fault of your own. It will help him again now. I have been working to this end for some years now. No doubt he has told you of his dream to make this home of his into a convalescent home for children? I have raised quite a lot of money and have already plans drawn up for altering the *Schloss* after my death. It will give Paul something to think about, and a new purpose, a new love.'

Harriet fought against the desire to weep. She said softly:

'I can see now why Paul loves you so much!'

The blue eyes smiled back at her from the twisted face. The one cool white hand she could move covered Harriet's where it lay taut on her lap.

'I, too, can see why he loves *you*, my dear. I have so often wondered about you . . . all these years hearing your name, yet never seeing even a picture of you. It seems to me a very terrible thing which your mother did. Paul told me, you know, how she effected your separation. Yet you found someone else.'

'I believed I was in love with my husband when I married him,' Harriet said. 'I was so lonely, and Tony was handsome, amusing and very attractive. I so desperately needed someone to love after Paul had gone out of my life. During those first years I strove very hard to make my marriage a success. I don't think Tony wanted quite so much loving. Then when my child was coming, I met Paul again. I didn't know he still loved me. I didn't know I still loved him. My whole being was concentrated on my unborn child. Afterwards, too, when Paul was so wonderful to me, I was still wrapped up in myself, my child, I never considered *him*. It was the same after Antonia died. I needed him, and he was there. It was

200

only as I began to get better that I realized I still loved him, and he told me he had never stopped loving me.'

'You stopped loving your husband?'

'I think I hated him!' Harriet said bitterly. 'I blamed him for my baby's death. I never wanted to see him again only . . .'

'Only what?' the quiet voice prompted her.

'I loved Paul, but I knew I couldn't go to him if I left Tony. Divorce . . . well, it is never very nice, but Tony threatened to cite Paul and I could not take that chance. Since then—well, I don't hate Tony now. He's so terribly sorry for what happened, and he's lonely and needs me. I have to stay with him, even though I can never love him again.'

'Now I understand everything,' the *Gräfin* said calmly. 'In this last letter, Paul told me you had said good-bye to one another. He told me of his great lasting love for you, but he never spoke of your love for him, only your need for his friendship. It was brave of you to keep the truth from him for I think if he knew you loved him he would throw up even his career for your happiness.'

'I believe that, too,' Harriet said. 'And that must never happen.'

'So each of us has a secret from him . . . a secret we guard for his good,' the *Gräfin* said gently. 'It is a link between us, my dear, that brings us close to one another although we have met only an hour ago.'

Harriet clasped the slim cold hand more tightly.

'You could never seem a stranger to me, *Madame*. I have known of you ever since I was a child of seventeen. I believed then that you would one day be my mother-in-law. And when I look into your eyes it is like looking at Paul.'

'You love him very much. It is a hard cross for one so young to bear. But you have already learned of suffering, Harriet, have you not? To lose one's baby is a terrible thing. Can you talk about it to me?'

'To you, yes!' Harriet said. 'But not now. You look tired and I feel sure you should rest. I'm going to take care of you, for Paul. Many years ago I wanted to be a nurse. Now I would like. to nurse you if you would let me.'

'My doctor has been trying to insist on a trained nurse, but I would not agree. I have no wish to spend my last days being ordered about.' There was a smile now around her mouth. 'Perhaps I shall have to give way at the end, but now—well, you will be just what I need, my dear. Your hands are so cool and soft. To feel them on my head as they are now brings me to the point of sleep.'

The voice became inaudible and as Harriet sat there she saw the old lady's eyes close and knew she must leave her now to rest.

She went back along the stone passage to her own room where the log-fire burned warm and comfortingly in the open fireplace. Then she pulled on the velvet bell-rope and sat down to wait for Maria.

The old peasant came shuffling along from her room at the end of the passage. Her vast black skirt and petticoats made a swish along the stone floors which halted outside Harriet's door. She knocked and was told to go in. She eyed the girl suspiciously, hoping that Harriet was not going to be the kind of guest who rang the bell at all hours of the day and night, wanting attention. She had quite enough to do with the cooking and caring for the *Gräfin*.

'You're wanting?' she said in halting English.

Harriet looked up at her and smiled.

'Only to talk to you, Maria. Can you spare me a few moments?'

She indicated another chair and, still suspicious, Maria lowered her bulky frame into it.

'To talk, *meine Frau*?'

'About the *Gräfin* and yourself, and my visit,' Harriet said, guessing that this might be difficult. Paul had spoken of Maria, the old woman who had once been his mother's personal maid in the days before the First World War when the *Schloss* had been filled with servants and luxurious living was at its height. After the Great War they had had to cut down expenses and Maria had become Paul's nurse until another war had sent him with his mother into hiding, and Maria, then

203

fifty, back to her home in the neighbouring village. When the *Gräfin* returned home after the armistice, there had been no money to reopen the whole *Schloss*—only the old kitchen and one or two of the bedrooms. Maria, ever faithful, had insisted on returning to act as cook, maid and companion to the *Gräfin* whom she guarded now like a faithful old bloodhound.

'The *Gräfin* is very ill,' Harriet said, seeing the look of acceptance and sorrow on the lined old face. 'I would like to talk to her doctor if you will give me his name.'

'You mean *Herr* Ricardstein? He comes himself from Vienna, whenever he can spare the time, to see the *Gräfin*. Tomorrow he will come again. He is an old family friend, you know.'

Harriet felt a flash of disappointment. She knew that these last minutes she had been hoping some local doctor had been in attendance and that a good specialist might yet be able to do something for Paul's mother. Now she knew that nothing could be done. If Vienna's leading doctor held no hope for her, then she, Harriet, would have to resign herself to the fact of the *Gräfin*'s death. But how soon? She had to know.

It did not seem strange to Harriet that she should mind so terribly about the death of someone she had only just met. Paul's mother, after the first shock of finding her bedridden

204

and partially paralysed, had seemed like an old friend; as close to her and certainly dearer to her than her own mother. Nor did it seem strange that she should be taking charge of the situation. She was acting instinctively as she knew Paul would act in her place.

'I will talk to *Herr* Ricardstein tomorrow,' she said. 'Now I would like to speak about your duties, Maria. You must find a great deal to do here in this big place by yourself.'

'I do not complain. The *Gräfin* does not like strangers here. *Doktor* Paul on his last visit wished his mother to employ more help, but I refused. I can manage alone.'

'Yes, but there will be more work with me staying here. I wondered if I might do a little to assist you, Maria. Perhaps I could sit with the *Gräfin* sometimes, read to her and look after her a little?'

Maria looked at her from beady brown eyes, eyes which broke into a sudden unexpected smile.

'Ah, this is why *Doktor* Paul sent you to us. Now I understand. He is too busy to come himself so he sends you. Is it not so?'

Clearly Maria felt it was Paul's place to be here.

'He is working hard, Maria, and his mother is very anxious he should not be interrupted in his studies. I should like to be a daughter to her while I am here.'

'This is *gut*!' Maria said, settling her work-worn hands comfortably across her ample lap. 'I do not see so well . . . to read the newspapers, you understand? I am often a little deaf and do not always hear the *Gräfin*'s bell. That is why I move here to the next room to better hear her in the night. Ah, *Fräulein*, she does not sleep much at night. It is not a good thing.'

'I'll talk to the doctor about it,' Harriet said quickly, appalled that the *Gräfin* should be so ill and so inadequately attended. How could *Herr* Ricardstein permit it?

The following day Harriet understood. Walking with *Herr* Ricardstein in the overgrown tangle of the once beautiful rose-garden, she asked her questions and was told the reason.

Herr Ricardstein was a small, rotund little man with a bald head and thick, horn-rimmed spectacles. He looked insignificant, but when he spoke the impression was of a great man, a strong one; and above all a man who was utterly sincere.

'Surely she should not be living here alone like this with only Maria?' Harriet said anxiously. 'I think Paul would be horrified if he knew.'

'Indeed, yes, young lady. Yet I think he, too, would appreciate the situation. The *Gräfin* has perhaps one, two, three months of life left. In her case this has not been a gradual illness. The first attack came without warning, was not very severe and did not give her much pain.

206

She told no one about it, and carried on as usual. But three months ago she had this second attack which paralysed her left side. She sent for me to come from Vienna then. I brought with me our best heart specialist. I think she suspected what was the truth. In any event, she gave him no chance to pretend. "Can you cure me, *Herr* Worfgan?" she asked him outright. "Yes or no?" He had to say he could not.'

The doctor shrugged his shoulders and looked at Harriet over the top of his spectacles.

' "If you cannot help me, no one can. How long have I to live?" she asked him. He told her the next attack would most probably be fatal, it would be likely to come within a year. You must let me write to Paul, I said, but she forbade me. "You must not betray a patient's symptoms to anyone," she said. "To another doctor," I began, but she cut me short. "In this case, it is not to another doctor, but to my son. He is not to be told until I say so." '

The man drew in his breath and sighed.

'We wanted to move her to hospital, but she would again not consider it. "It is my life . . . what is left of it, *Herr Doktor*. I will end it in the way I choose." Well, she is right, of course, and there are many such who prefer to die at home. All the same, there is much that could be done in hospital to ease the pain. I told her so, but she is a brave woman and would not

207

listen to me. "When I no longer know who I am or what I am, then you can do as you please," she told me. "Until then, I will do as I please." It is not easy for me, as you will understand, *Fräulein*. I was friendly all my life with her husband. Paul is my protégé, and I am as fond of him as if he were my son. Yet there is nothing I can do—nothing. I have given her drugs to ease the pain. Thank God it is not too bad yet. Sometimes it is so, although I am afraid she will suffer when the end comes.'

'And when will that be?' Harriet asked.

'It is difficult to be sure. It could be tomorrow, or not for some months. I cannot say.'

'But why so soon? What makes you so sure it will be so soon?' Harriet asked desperately.

The doctor looked at her sympathetically.

'You have not met the *Gräfin* before, *Fräulein*. When first she came to me she was a commanding figure of a woman, five feet ten—yes, tall for a woman; Paul is like her— and her face, for all she endured in the war, was as beautiful as that of a girl of twenty. You can see for yourself how this terrible disease has brought about its destruction. Only her eyes are the same . . . and her mind. Her will and determination are unchanged.'

'Surely she should have a nurse at least? A trained nurse?'

The doctor smiled, a hint of admiration mixing with exasperation in his tone.

'She has told me again today that if I engage a nurse, she will forbid her entrance to her room. I cannot force her to accept, and in such cases I prefer that she should have things as she wishes. Of course, the local village nurse comes twice a day to wash her and see to her needs. All the same, I am more than relieved that you are here, young lady. Maria, loyal though she is, is getting old and deaf. I shall leave the *Gräfin* in your charge.'

Harriet was suddenly afraid.

'But I am not a nurse. How shall I know when to call you? I don't know anything about heart diseases.'

The doctor put a hand on her arm.

'At present she is in full command of her senses. When the attack comes you will not fail to know it. Do you understand?'

'And Paul? Must he wait until then?' Harriet cried.

'Unless she will permit you to tell him before. It will not be easy for him, and she knows this. She is a very brave woman and I think she would deny herself her last sight of her own son if she could avoid distressing him. All the same, I think he would prefer to be here and you might add your persuasions to mine to see if she will agree.'

When the doctor had gone, Harriet went back to her own room to sit and think for a while before she returned to the sick-room. For the first time in months she had no thought for herself or her own problems. Thrown into this totally unexpected and frightening whirlpool of disaster, she could think only of the old lady and of Paul. Perhaps it would be easier to die than to have to face the look of horror and distress in the eyes of someone you loved. Yet she must need her son . . . long for him quite desperately, knowing she might die suddenly and never see him again. How had any woman the courage to go on writing as she had done, telling Paul about the change in the weather, the carnival Maria had said they'd had in the village, the skiers who had stopped to see over the *Schloss* on their way up the mountain for the sport? How could she have written to Harriet, as she had done, saying:

I am afraid you will find it rather quiet and a little dull here after life in London. But Paul tells me you need rest and sunshine so maybe you would not be bored. It would be quite possible, for you to go ski-ing further up the mountain where there is still plenty of snow.

It will be nice to see you for Paul has so often spoken of you and I hope you will stay for some time . . .

She had had no idea, suspicion, nor inner warning of what to expect.

An hour later Paul's mother was apologizing

to her.

'It was very selfish of me to agree to your coming here at such a time. I had no right to let you come, especially since you were not well yourself. But this has been my only weakness. I did so very much want to see you, my dear. It was because my son loved you— still loves you—because he wanted you to be here. I knew you would have seen him, would perhaps talk about him a little and bring him closer to me. I never knew, of course, that you loved him.'

'Oh, *Madame*,' Harriet said earnestly. 'Won't you let me write and tell him? I know you want to spare him the agony of seeing you so ill. But think of it from his point of view. How will he feel when he does discover the truth? He will never forgive himself for not being near you when you needed him most. He will never forgive me for not telling him.'

'You may tell him that I forbade you,' the old lady said with her gentle smile. 'He knows I am not lightly gainsaid.'

'But it isn't fair to him!' Harriet cried.

'I will let him come before I die,' was the calm reply. 'But it may be some time yet, and to tell you the truth, Harriet dear, now you are here I feel I can wait more calmly and happily for the end. If Paul were here I should have to worry constantly because I know what agony such waiting would be for him. I would have to pretend I was strong even when I felt weak. I would have to hide the moments of pain from him. So you see, I am not entirely selfless. If I can see him just once before I die I shall have all I want.'

Harriet recognized defeat and did not bring up the subject again.

CHAPTER TWELVE

Maria's weatherbeaten old face was creased in smiles so that it resembled more than ever an old walnut.

'She is much better, *Fräulein*, I know it. Last night so much sleep and today her eyes shining and her voice strong like ever it was. It is you, *Fräulein,* who have done this.'

Harriet shook her head, knowing that there was really very little she had been able to do to help the *Gräfin*. Yet she had to admit that there did seem an improvement in her condition—an improvement that had begun with her own arrival four days ago. Knowing nothing whatever about heart troubles she, like Maria, had suddenly begun to hope, despite the specialist's statement, that another attack might not come for years. She was waiting impatiently now for *Herr* Ricardstein's next visit so that she could hear her own hopes confirmed.

Meanwhile, Paul's mother insisted that

Harriet should go out more.

'Paul wished *me* to take care of *you*, dear child,' she said with her twisted smile. 'So to please me I would like you to arrange a few days' ski-ing up in the mountains. I have some friends called Hauffman who have a winter chalet in Bichlalon. I would be pleased if you would telephone them and tell them I would be grateful if they would look after you. They will, I know, be delighted to have you.'

'Oh, no?' Harriet protested. 'I would really prefer to stay here with you. It's years since I went ski-ing. I haven't done so since I was at school in Paris.'

'All the same. Harriet'—she pronounced it Harri*ette* just as Paul always did, Harriet thought—'I wish you to go, to put some colour into your cheeks and to give you an appetite. Maria tells me you eat nothing.'

So Harriet had agreed to go and had telephoned the Hauffmans. Acting on instructions, she had kept secret the *Gräfin*'s illness and merely said she was indisposed.

Frau Hauffman had been delighted. In her broken English she said:

'A friend of Paul's will at our house most welcome be. Paul and my son, Karl, for many years friends have been. Karl is home now and will be pleased to have a young *Fräulein* to entertain. You tomorrow come, yes? You take the morning train to Kitzbühel and then the aerial cable railway to Bichlalon. This end we

213

will meet you.'

Harriet had packed her ski-ing clothes as Paul had told her there would still be snow on the mountains near his home. As she dressed in them she was surprised to find how well they fitted her. The tight, dark green trousers were becoming to her long, slim legs, and the thick white fisherman's knit jersey seemed to bring out the green of her eyes and the slight tan she had recently acquired in the Austrian sunshine. Pulling on the zip-up ski-jacket, she went to say good-bye to Paul's mother.

'You look very young and very pretty,' the *Gräfin* told her. 'I expect young Karl will fall very much in love with you. He is always falling in love, but it is never very serious with him. A charming boy, Harriet, you will like him.'

Harriet kissed the *Gräfin*'s hand and smoothed back the pillows.

'You are sure you will be all right?'

'Of course, my dear. Now run along and enjoy yourself. I shall look forward to hearing all the details when you get back. You have Paul's skis? And rucksack?'

'Yes, thank you. And a warm dress to wear in the evening. Now I must hurry. Maria says the taxi is waiting already.'

The rickety old Mercedes that had brought her up from the village wound its way slowly down the hill towards the village. The sun was shining with considerable warmth and Harriet felt a sudden lifting of her spirits. Spring was

214

already here in the valley, the beginning of another year. Soon the gentians would be out and the wild flowers were already showing their buds above the wet grass verge of the roadside.

Here Paul was a boy, she thought dreamily. He probably played amongst those fir trees with Karl, and built dams across that little waterfall.

There was a wonderful feeling of nearness to Paul; a proximity that defied the hundreds of miles which separated them. Today she would be walking in his footsteps, for the *Gräfin* had told her how often Paul made this same journey for a weekend in the mountains with Karl Hauffman. She held Paul's skis—too long for her but usable—and carried his rucksack. It was almost as if he were there in person, sitting beside her.

In the village the local people were busy about their day's work. One woman, dressed in a peasant's long black skirts, was pegging out her washing. Another sat by her kitchen door milking a goat, while a tiny, pinafore-clad child played in the mud, its small bare bottom upturned innocently to the warmth of the sun. At the neat little station, another young mother stood waiting for the train, a baby wrapped in a shawl across her back.

Harriet felt her heart miss a beat. She was drawn towards the woman and her child as if invisible hands were beckoning to her. Until

215

this moment she had always walked away from any baby, unable to bear the memory of Antonia.

As she tried in vain to see the tiny face, the mother turned and smiled and spoke in a *patois* Harriet did not understand. Harriet smiled back and shook her head, then put out her hand to point to the child.

Immediately the girl unwrapped the shawl and handed the baby trustingly to Harriet.

She could not tell if it were a boy or girl. She knew only that it was small and helpless and not at all like her baby had been. As she handed the baby back to its mother she realized with surprise that it had not hurt her to hold the child. The hardness had melted and left her heart free. She could remember Antonia now with sadness but without that aching pain.

Paul was right after all when he said time would soften the pain.

She wished she could converse with this girl, tell her about the baby she had lost. But they could understand nothing but each other's smiles.

Presently Harriet's train arrived and she was sitting on the hard wooden seat, among a crowd of other young holidaymakers, most, like herself, carrying skis and rucksacks. One young man had an accordion, which he played very well all the way to Kitzbühel, the young men and women with him joining in the songs

216

they all seemed to know. Harriet was drawn into the group despite her shyness for she could not understand their Austrian German. She listened with delight to the singing and thought what a pity it was that there were no occasions like this in England. Much as she loved the country of her birth, something in her warmed towards this lovely mountain land where the sun shone and everyone seemed so happy and full of life and laughter.

It's Paul's country, she told herself with a smile, for she could not help but love everything that had made him the man he was.

She was thrilled again by the aerial cable railway that took her swinging up into air towards the snow-topped mountains. For over five thousand feet the cable carried her, nervous but enchanted by the aerial view of the Wirn and valley below, by the rugged rocky mountainsides and dark green tops of the fir forests far beneath her.

Karl Hauffman was waiting with a horse and sleigh at the terminus. Somehow Harriet had no difficulty in recognizing him. His sun-burned, attractive face was wreathed in smiles and a cheeky red woollcn cap topped the mass of dark curly hair that fell over his forehead. The twinkling brown eyes were exactly as the *Gräfin* had described them.

'You must be Harriet,' he said, stepping towards her and kissing her hand . . . a Continental touch which Harriet liked very much. 'I did not know what to expect, of course, but I knew Paul would not choose anything but a pretty girl.'

'Please!' Harriet said quickly, fearing a misunderstanding. 'Paul is . . . that is, I'm not a girl. I'm a married woman. Paul is just an old friend.'

The young man grinned cheerfully.

'Then I am delighted anew for I would not want to tread on Paul's toes. A married woman, but at least you have not your husband with you. So I nominate myself your escort!'

Harriet smiled back. Karl's outspokenness was clear indication that she need not worry about him. He just could not resist flirting with any woman, but he meant no harm by it.

As she climbed into the sleigh beside him and watched his strong muscular arms sling her skis in beside his own, she thought how happy she was. Strange that she could be happy again—and without Paul. There must be something about the cocktail of sun and snow and mountain air that was intoxicating. It would be impossible not to enjoy herself in such surroundings. The road was no more than a track beaten down by horses' hooves, skis and sleighs. The snow lay deep and crisp all around them and sparkled like glass in the sunshine. Against the carpet of crystal white, the skiers' brightly coloured clothes gave a Christmas-card impression of brilliance and gaiety. Their shouts echoed round the sleigh, mingling with the harness bells, and two small boys clung impudently to the back of Karl's sleigh, snatching a free ride, their faces grinning cheekily as Harriet caught sight of them.

'The ski-ing is very good,' Karl told her. 'Hard and fast. Already this morning I have made two runs down to Kitzbühel. Perhaps after lunch you will come with me?'

'I think I'd better have some practice runs on the nursery slopes first,' Harriet said quickly. 'I haven't ski'd for eight years. I don't even know if I shall be able to stand up!'

Karl clicked his tongue at the horse and turned to Harriet, saying with a laugh:

'It is like the bicycling; once you have learnt you never quite forget. All the same, a little practice is perhaps good for today. I will give you . . . how do you call it? . . . the refresher course.'

'Your English is very good,' Harriet told him. 'You have been to England?'

'No, but to America. After the war I went there for four years to take an engineering degree at Harvard. I was fortunate to have an aunt married to an American and she arranged it for me. I like America very much. Perhaps I shall marry an American girl and go back to live there.'

It soon became clear to Harriet that the Hauffmans had plenty of money. She wondered how this came about since people

219

like Paul's parents had lost everything they possessed in the war. But Karl told her later that his father had foreseen the war, just as Paul's father had done, and had sent most of his money to America before the German invasion.

'We were very poor during the war,' Karl said, shrugging his shoulders, 'but let's not think about those days. It is over now and I'm glad to say we have our money back. This is just our winter holiday home, Harriet. In Vienna we have a big house where life is very entertaining. You must come to visit us there for we often have parties and the house is always full of people.'

Harriet wondered just how beautiful Karl's home must be, for the chalet was furnished with as much taste and as expensively as the average English country house. Her own room had a charming little wooden balcony, common to all chalets, and her bed was well sprung and covered with a mountainous eiderdown which kept her beautifully warm. There was also a deep, comfortable armchair and a small antique desk, a washbasin and a thick-piled carpet, none of it in the least as she had expected a mountain 'hut' to be!

At lunch she met *Herr* and *Frau* Hauffman and the other two guests, a girl about her own age whose name seemed to be Nina and her fiancé, a tall, fair Swede called Olaf. They all spoke English for Harriet's benefit and Karl spent most of the time teasing the girl, Nina, who just laughed at him from eyes as dark brown and flirtatious as his own. Harriet discovered later that she was really called Christina and was one of Karl's numerous girl cousins.

His mother and father were charming. *Frau* Hauffman was very elegant, as so many Austrians were, and it was obvious where Karl got his dark hair and eyes and good looks. Although she must be nearing sixty, she was still a very attractive woman. *Herr* Hauffman was round and fat and jolly and vied with his son in paying Harriet wild and extravagant compliments.

It was all very light-hearted and when she went to bed that night Harriet was ashamed to recall that she had barely given Paul's mother a thought all day. Now, as she settled down to sleep, tired from her afternoon ski-ing and the big evening dinner of venison, she wondered how she was, if the improvement had continued and whether there could indeed be hope of a longer lease of life for her, if not a complete recovery.

The following morning Harriet was woken by the successive thuds of half a dozen snowballs on her window. As she climbed out of bed and went sleepily to the balcony, a rush of cold air jolted her awake and simultaneously she felt the warmth of the sun striking her face. Then Karl's voice called up to her.

'Come on, sleepy-head. How about a run before breakfast? It's lovely.'

Like a young girl again, Harriet hurried into her ski-ing clothes and within ten minutes had joined Karl in the snow. Except for lipstick, she left her face free of make-up and the result was very attractive.

Karl wasted no time telling her so.

'It really is the greatest shame you are a *Frau* and not a *Fräulein,* Harriet. I find you so very pretty that I could make the pass at you with no difficulty!'

'Make *a* pass!' Harriet laughed at him. 'And that's an American phrase—one we don't use much in England.'

'What matter! You understand me. Now tell me of this husband of yours, Harriet. How comes it he lets you here alone and unchaperoned? I would not risk such a thing if you were my wife.'

'Oh, Englishmen are very trusting,' Harriet parried the question. But Karl insisted.

'Then it is not right they should be. I think I will have to kiss you once or twice to teach him the lesson.'

Harriet gathered a handful of snow and threw it at him.

'You called me down here to go ski-ing,' she reminded him.

Karl laughed.

'Yes, well, we will go. Today I think you can

222

manage the run. You are the good skier, Harriet, for you have balance and that is the most important thing.'

'But I'm so stiff!' Harriet laughed. 'I don't think I can come down that steep run, Karl.'

'I will stay beside you and you will be quite safe,' Karl told her. 'Now let us go quickly. It is almost nine o'clock.'

The run, though difficult, was within Harriet's capabilities, especially as Karl, true to his word, stayed beside her, advising her what to expect of the various turns and twists, stopping frequently to give her plenty of breaks, pointing out the view, which was magnificent, overlooking as it did the whole range of mountains and the villages, tiny and remote, nestling at the foot of each range.

'See there, to your left, Harriet? That is the village near the von Murrens' home. You cannot see the *Schloss*, for it lies behind that pine forest. I have often stood here with Paul trying to see the smoke from the chimneys when we were boys. Those were happy days before the war.'

It was the first time Karl had ever spoken seriously. Quite suddenly, he said:

'My sister, Lotte, would be with us, too. She was my twin. I used to think one day when we were grown up she might marry Paul. But it was not to be.'

Harriet waited, not wanting to ask him what had happened to this clearly well-loved sister.

223

But Karl went on, saying: 'The Russians took her when she was sixteen. We never saw her again. After the war, we discovered she had died from tuberculosis somewhere near Moscow. I think this was when Paul first conceived the idea of his clinic. I hope it will one day come about. He has promised to call the first ward Lotte.'

Harriet was appalled by the revelation. It gave her a new outlook on Karl. He had seemed to her so carefree and untouched by tragedy. Now she knew that beneath the lighthearted exterior, he, too, had suffered. Maybe everyone had their deep-hidden sorrows, she thought, suddenly ashamed of her own outward expressions of grief. Karl did not inflict others with his sadness as she had done. It must sometimes have seemed to Paul that she had made a terrible fuss over the loss of one baby when he had seen the death of hundreds amongst the refugees; had known personally young girls like Karl's sister, taken from their homes to some dreadful, only half-guessed fate.

'I have distressed you,' Karl said, seeing the tears in her eyes. 'I should not have spoken.'

'No, I'm glad you did, Karl. You see I, too, have had a great loss in my life. It's really why I am here. Last year I lost my baby in an accident. I thought I didn't want to go on living and I'm ashamed now because I made no effort to hide my feelings from others. It was, I see now, only one small tragedy amongst millions, and I had no right to concentrate so on my grief.'

Karl took her hand and pressed it in a quick, friendly gesture.

'I guessed something unhappy about you,' he said. 'It was the expression in your eyes . . . so sad and lost and lonely. Only when I try hard can I bring laughter to them and then it makes me happy, too. You must try not to be sad, Harriet. When you smile, you are most beautiful!'

They did not speak so intimately again but that brief conversation made them firm friends. And Harriet had learned a lesson from Karl . . . to think less of herself and more of trying to make others happy. She could even think of Tony more kindly, remembering the good things about him, forgetting the bad. He had Karl's carefree nature, and like Karl, he might conceal beneath it, a deeper and more sensitive side to his nature.

Perhaps I don't really know Tony at all, Harriet told herself as the train took her slowly back to the village at the end of her brief stay. Perhaps he's really the man he seemed to be when we last spoke of our marriage. Then Tony had been gentle, loving, repentant, anxious only to win her back and gain her forgiveness.

A letter from him awaited her return to the *Schloss*. She took it to her room and read his

225

broad, rather untidy handwriting with mixed feelings.

My dearest Harriet,

I hope you are having a good time and enjoying your holiday, also that you are beginning to feel better and happier. It has been very lonely here without you and time passes slowly. I've been in to the office a few times but, as you know, there's nothing much doing there to keep me occupied. Sometimes I think I ought to get a decent job where I'm forced to do some hard work. Yet there isn't much I can do, having no talents or training for anything else.

I've also been out a couple of times but I don't seem able to enjoy myself with you away. I know I promised not to ask you to come back before the three weeks are up but if I go on feeling this way I'll be tempted to join you out there. Of course I couldn't very well stay at von Murren's home, but perhaps we could go somewhere together?

I have only had one postcard from you telling me of your arrival. It would be wonderful to have a letter.

The laundry hasn't been collected since you left, and I've had to buy two new shirts. If you tell me how to get hold of them, I'll give them a ring and chivvy them up.

From your loving husband,

Tony.

226

Harriet felt both frightened and guilty. First and foremost she did not want Tony out here yet. He couldn't know about Paul's mother, of course, but she, Harriet, could certainly not leave her while things were as they were, not even if Tony needed her. At the same time, she could have written to him and explained the situation.

She sat down on the impulse and hurriedly wrote a reply. She told him of her recent skiing holiday in detail. Then, more slowly, she told him about Paul's mother.

. . . the doctor comes again tomorrow and I am hoping so much that he will change his opinion. She really does seem so much better. I know it will seem strange to you that I should be so concerned about someone who is virtually a stranger to me, Tony, but you would understand if you knew her. She is so sweet and so brave. She is terribly grateful for everything I do for her—which isn't much, I'm afraid—and never once have I heard her complain.

I just have to stay here for the time being and until I know what is happening, I cannot make any plans for the future. But you will be glad to know I am better both in health and in myself. I can even bring myself to talk of Antonia now and not to want to cry every time I see another baby.

Please be patient a little longer, Tony, and you will find that I am not ungrateful. I am sorry I didn't write before but I will do so regularly now. By the way, it's the South London Laundry Service and they are in the phone book but don't be too angry or they'll stop calling and you know how difficult it is to get a good service now! . . .

Her pen came to a halt as she neared the end of her letter. Tony had signed himself *Your loving husband,* yet she could not bring herself to write in turn *Your loving wife.* Her heart still belonged to Paul. Finally, she signed herself *Affectionately, Harriet.* One could not, after all, discard so lightly eight years of married life, she told herself. Simple, domestic details like the laundry held people together despite their differences.

Harriet brought her thoughts to a halt as she began to consider the future. She was not yet ready for that. If Tony would only leave her alone a while longer, she might grow fond of him again just as this last week had taught her to forgive him.

CHAPTER THIRTEEN

The *Gräfin* welcomed her back warmly, and Harriet was delighted to see that the old lady seemed stronger, more full of vitality than when she had left.

When she congratulated Harriet on her glowing cheeks and newly acquired sun-tan, telling her how well she looked after her few days in the mountains, Harriet was able to say truthfully:

'You look so much better, too, *Madame*. You, too, have colour in your cheeks!'

The *Gräfin* smiled.

'Yes, I feel much better again today. I think you must have given me a new lease of life, Harriet. I have been lying here thinking about you and I have been looking forward to hearing of your holiday. How are the Hauffmans? How is dear Karl? Sit here beside me and tell me about it.'

But Harriet's hopes were dashed to the ground when *Herr* Ricardstein arrived next day.

'I am afraid this quite often happens. You must not raise your hopes,' he said. 'Patients seem to take a turn for the better, but I am afraid it cannot mean more than a temporary improvement. You must try not to let it distress you too deeply. She suffers quite a lot

229

of pain and it will be a release for her when the end comes.'

'She never complains,' Harriet cried. 'One wouldn't know she was suffering at all.'

'That is because she is proud and will not let you see. She knows it would upset you. Now, young lady, I have two things to ask you. First, could you try to persuade the *Gräfin* to let you engage this nurse? She really must have professional attendance; someone who can be trusted with the medicines and drugs she requires. If necessary, you must tell the white lie and say neither you nor Maria care to take the responsibility and would yourselves be happier. She must have a nurse.'

'I'll try to make her understand,' Harriet said. 'What else, Doctor?'

'I've been reconsidering, and I think it is time Paul knew the truth. The attack might come at any time and we want Paul here before that happens. No matter what she may feel about it now, if we wait until she asks for him, it may be too late.'

Harriet's thoughts bridged the hundreds of miles between them as she realized what an appalling shock this would be for Paul.

'I know this will not be easy for him,' the doctor said, reading her expression. 'I think it would be best if first you wrote to say his mother has had a slight heart attack, that I am here in attendance and will be writing to him. Your letter will then prepare him a little for

230

the news I shall have to give him in my letter. But you must not stress the seriousness of her condition too much for I wish him to remain in London until he hears the truth from me. He must prepare himself so that when he does arrive, he will be better able to conceal from his mother how much he is affected.'

'I understand. I'll write this afternoon,' Harriet said.

It was the most difficult letter she had ever had to compose. She wanted so much to be able to offer him the comfort of her own love for him, but she could not do it. She had promised Tony she would not see or write to Paul. Circumstances required her to break that promise but she could at least make it factual without being personal.

After she had posted it, she went to her room and gave way to tears. That she should have to be the one to give Paul such news! She well knew the kind of turmoil into which her letter would throw him and how anxiously he would be waiting for the even worse news in *Herr* Ricardstein's letter.

It suddenly hit Harriet like a physical blow that within a week at the most, Paul would be here. She had never thought to see him again and had intended never to do so. For her to be here when he came would only add to his unhappiness and she knew suddenly that she must go quickly before he arrived. If she stayed, she would not have the strength to keep her true feelings from him.

Hurriedly, she dried her eyes, her mind made up that the moment Paul wired the time of his arrival, she would depart. But first she knew she must make arrangements for a nurse to come.

Strangely enough, Paul's mother made no objection when Harriet told her she really felt they would all be happier with a trained nurse in residence. Once so adamant against the idea, she now acquiesced with a calm acceptance, saying:

'If you would prefer it, Harriet dear, I will not oppose you. *Herr* Ricardstein told me he had a new drug he wished me to take and that it was dangerous for an untrained girl to handle it. I quite see that you would not want the responsibility. All the same, dear child, I would have had the utmost confidence in you. You have the gentle touch and understanding of a born nurse.'

Paul had once said the same thing. Perhaps, after all this, it would not be too late to take her training. Tony might object, but it would give her something to do and some aim in her life, now there was no baby. If she qualified, it would at least mean that she could nurse if ever an occasion such as this arose in her life again. Impulsively she told the *Gräfin*, and was delighted to hear the old lady give her blessing to the idea.

'It will help you to forget your loss, and at

the same time it will keep you happy and occupied. And the training will never come amiss.

Somehow, sitting beside the *Gräfin*, talking to her about her own future, of Paul's clinic and the American girl's interest in it, of the Hauffmans, it was impossible to realize that this wonderful, brave woman was so close to death. But the following day, the *Gräfin*'s condition became suddenly worse. In the early hours of the morning, Harriet heard her bell ring and found her in great pain.

Fortunately, it was only an hour or two before the local village nurse arrived in a taxi and was able to give her the necessary injections to ease it. As she lay on the point of sleep, the *Gräfin* turned her head slowly towards Harriet and said slowly:

'You know, dear child, I really would like to see Paul. Would it be very wrong, do you think, to ask him to come? I did so want to spare him but ...'

Her voice trailed away as the drug took effect. Harriet looked at the nurse in a sudden panic, she said: 'It won't be too late, will it? She isn't ... isn't dying now?'

Each time she sat beside the great four-poster, Harriet wondered if this would be her last sight of the woman she had grown in so short a while to love and to respect. She still intended to go away the moment Paul's telegram came in answer to her own

233

announcing the time of his arrival; but Fate again took charge of her life. Paul did not wire, but arrived at the *Schloss* in person.

Hearing the taxi, believing it to be *Herr* Ricardstein, Harriet ran down the wide staircase to pull open the great studded door. All colour drained from her face as she saw Paul, his own face white and strained.

'Harriet!' He took her arms and his eyes searched her face. 'What's been happening? My mother—how is she? Is the doctor here? How bad is it? I must know what's happening.'

His frantic questions brought her back to sudden calmness.

'Come into the drawing-room, Paul. I'll try to explain everything.'

'I must see her first,' Paul said, but she held him back by physical force.

'You can't see her looking the way you do, Paul. You must pull yourself together first. You look terrible.'

Indeed he did. The worry and his desperate rush to get here without a moment's loss of time had made him forget his appearance. Usually so impeccably neat and tidy, his tweed suit was now crumpled, his shirt collar creased, his fair hair curling down untidily over the anxious lines of his forehead.

She led him into the sitting-room where a pine-log fire blazed in the huge fireplace.

'I'll tell Maria to make you some coffee,' she said, as he lowered himself into a chair. 'Your mother is sleeping now, so you won't want to disturb her just yet.'

She returned a moment or two later, and seated herself opposite him. Briefly, without sentiment, she answered his questions.

'But why, *why* didn't you send for me sooner? I'd a right to know. I'm her son. How could you have done such a thing, Harriet . . . you, of all people!'

'Paul, it was *her wish*!'

Some of the tenseness left his face.

'Yet you must have known I would want to be here, despite everything. I can believe she would try to spare me, but you should have known I would rather not be spared.'

She looked at him compassionately from those wide, green eyes.

'Paul, it was to spare herself, too. She would hate to see you suffering on her behalf. It would be as hard for her to endure as her own pain. She loves you so much. This sacrifice was the last thing she could do for you.'

Paul remained silent, his emotions unbearable. Harriet watched his changing expressions, her own face naked with her distress for him, her love for him. If she were only free to go to him now, to try to offer him what little comfort there was . . .

He looked up suddenly and saw her expression. His face softened.

'At least *you* were here, Harriet. You must have been a great comfort to her. She wrote to

235

me, you know, and told me how much she liked you . . . loved you. She said that to have you here with her was like suddenly discovering a long-lost daughter.'

Tears filled Harriet's eyes.

'I love her, too, Paul,' she said unsteadily. 'I shall hate leaving her.'

'Leaving her?' Paul jerked out the words, his eyes startled. 'You're not—you're not going away—not *now*?'

'Paul, I *must* go!' she said uncertainly. 'Don't you see that I can't stay any longer? I've no place here, and . . .' her voice broke.

'You can't go, Harriet. You must realise how much I'm going to need you.'

'Oh, Paul!' Harriet whispered. 'That's why I have to go away. I gave Tony my word I wouldn't ever see you again. That was one of the conditions of my coming here at all. If I stay . . .'

'Perhaps you're right, Harriet,' Paul said flatly. 'I've no right to ask you to remain here.'

'Paul, it isn't because you have no right to ask me!' She had to make him understand. *'It's because I love you!'*

The words were out in the stress of the moment, her determination never to utter them obviated by the more urgent wish to offer him some comfort in understanding. 'I've loved you for months, Paul. Perhaps I never stopped loving you. That's why Tony was so jealous of you. He guessed, and I admitted the

236

truth to him. I want to stay here with you more than I've ever wanted anything in the whole world. But I promised . . . for all our sakes.'

Paul stared across the brief space that separated them. Her words had momentarily stunned him. He had grown used to his own unrequited love for her but to learn of her love for him was like receiving a draft of water in an arid desert.

The silence became unbearable as each felt the desperate need for closer proximity. Yet they sat there, Paul slowly realizing the powerlessness of his position. He had never needed her love more than he did now at this crisis in his life. Yet now he had as little right as ever to accept what she alone could give him just by her presence here. Her promise to Tony was as binding on him as it was on her. And she was *Tony's wife*, not his.

'I shouldn't have asked you—I didn't know . . .' he began awkwardly. Then, suddenly determined, he said: 'Don't you see, Harriet, what a difference this makes to everything? When last we talked about ourselves I didn't know you loved me. I felt I had no right to come between a husband and wife. But now it's different. There is no point in ruining three people's lives. Let Tony divorce you, Harriet, and stay here with me.'

Harriet clenched her hands in her lap.

'Nothing is different, Paul. Don't you see what would happen? Tony would name you,

237

and you would most certainly be struck off the medical register. It would be the end of your career!'

'I'd give it up willingly, for you,' Paul said. But even as he spoke he knew how terrible such a thing would be for him. It would mean the end of his life's work, and the end of his hopes to turn his home into a clinic under his care. Yet he *would* forsake it all for the reward of Harriet's love.

'I believe you, Paul. But I love you too much to let you do such a thing. A doctor's life is not really his own. It belongs to humanity, and there is so much you can do—already do—for other people. I could not take you from them. You know I'm right, Paul; you know in your heart that there is no hope for us.'

'But, Harriet, I love you . . . I need you—'

'Paul, don't!' she broke in tremulously. 'I'm weak enough as it is. Help me to be strong. Let's think of your mother and how willingly she sacrificed herself all her life for you and your career. It is only a small thing for us to give up for the same goal. She believes in you, and so do I. You know you are going to do great and wonderful things. That will be our compensation, Paul, together with the fact that we shall retain our integrity.'

The mention of his mother brought Paul back to sanity in the way Harriet had hoped for. He had never in his life done anything he might have been afraid to tell his mother, yet

238

he knew it would break her heart if he were to tell her he was abandoning his career in order to acquire another man's wife. Although she was so modern in her outlook on most things, he knew she was sufficiently old-fashioned not to think easily of condoning divorce.

'All right, Harriet. I won't try to persuade you to do anything we know is wrong. If you feel you must go, I won't try to stop you. But if you could stay . . . just . . . just until the end . . . You could trust me. I give you my word. I'll never try to touch you or to speak of my love for you. Can't you trust yourself, Harriet?'

It was a test she had not considered. In the past she had succeeded until now in hiding her true feelings from Paul. It had given her the strength to say good-bye to him once. Now she had declared her love and it would not be so easy. Yet perhaps for his sake she could stamp on her emotions and be no more to him than another person around the house. If the mere fact of her presence comforted him, she could stay here. Tony would surely understand if she gave him the facts of the matter.

'I'll write to Tony today,' she said quietly. 'If he has no objection, then I'll stay, Paul.'

While Paul sat with his mother, desperately trying to keep from her his shock at her appearance, his anxiety, his pity, his fear, Harriet sat in her own room struggling with her letter to her husband.

. . . It cannot be long now, Tony, or she would not have sent for Paul. It is a terrible thing to have to watch someone dying this way, in pain. It is worst of all for Paul who loves his mother so dearly.

He wants me to stay on a little longer partly because it will be a relief for him to have someone to talk to (there is only the nurse and old Maria here other than myself) and partly because his mother often asks for me.

I know you won't much like the idea, Tony, but please try to understand. I give you my solemn promise once again that nothing will pass between Paul and myself to which you could have even the slightest objection. If I stay, it will be in the capacity of a family friend, no more. I have never broken my word to you, Tony, so if I say you can trust me, you can believe it to be true.

If you cannot bring yourself to see why I want to stay, I will come back. I don't mean this to be a kind of moral blackmail but if you can give me your sympathy and understanding now, it will make all the difference in the world to our future together.

Was it too much to ask, she wondered, as she sealed down the envelope and walked slowly down through the trees to post it. Tony

240

knew she loved Paul, knew Paul loved her. Was she being unreasonable in hoping that he would grant them the support each could give the other while death approached? Would Tony fully understand the shock this was to Paul? Hc had never cared a great deal for his own parents. All the same, he must have loved someone well enough to judge how terrible it would be to see them dying by degrees.

If only she could believe in Tony's deeper nature. His way of loving seemed so less intense than hers or Paul's. Perhaps he really had loved their baby, but had not been able to show it as she did. Yet Tony was not an introvert. Far from it. He said he loved her, Harriet. Would that love allow him to give her this respite? Or was Tony's loving all take and possession?

How little I really know about the man I married, Harriet thought. I know far more about Paul. There had been so many different Tonys; the irresponsible, pleasure-loving boy; the sulky, bad-tempered man when he was found out. How hurt she had been to discover Tony's physical unfaithfulness to her! The proud, excited father; the repentant Tony after Antonia's death; the incredibly cruel, jealous, angry man who had threatened Paul; and lastly, the loving, pleading, anxious husband who wanted his wife back. Which was the real Tony? Were they all part of the whole?

She wanted to understand him and to know

241

him as he really was. Yet because she had seen so many different facets of his character over the years, she found herself unable to trust her own judgment of him, knowledge of him. He wasn't a bad man, she was sure of that. Weak, perhaps, and irresponsible, but not really unkind or cruel. Surely now he would show himself in his best light and not let himself be a prey to jealousy without cause.

Yet it wasn't really without cause, Harriet told herself honestly. Even without any physical expression, whenever she and Paul were together, their love for one another bridged the space between them with invisible bonds. Their minds reached out and touched in mutual understanding even while their hands remained still at their sides. Tony had every right to resent their being together, for it meant an unspoken intimacy that was the very expression of love.

Harriet reached the point where she was willing to admit that Tony had some grounds for not being happy about her staying on at the *Schloss* now Paul was here. She could admit that it was her love for Paul that made her want to stay by him when he most needed her, not a mere friendly gesture. Their love was based as much on a mental need as a physical one and it was possible to be mentally unfaithful.

If Tony objects, I'll go home, Harriet thought again. My first duty is to the man I married and, no matter what it costs me, I must resign myself to leaving Paul if I have to.

She heard Paul's voice calling her and with a little sigh she went slowly along the corridor to the *Gräfin*'s room.

CHAPTER FOURTEEN

Tony was in a burning rage. He felt Harriet had cheated him in some way he could not fully comprehend but which left him angry and resentful. Admittedly she could not have known von Murren's mother was so ill; admittedly under different circumstances Paul would not have gone home. But seeing he had had to do so, Harriet might at least have had the decency to leave him to manage his own affairs.

All that nonsense in her letter about Paul needing her! What about him, Tony? He needed her too. And she was *his* wife. Anyone would think Paul was the husband and he, Tony, the lover. Well, he told himself with bitterness, it would have to come to an end. He'd stood enough of Harriet's high-sounding moral letters asking him to be patient and understanding and sympathetic. He didn't think much of psychological and sentimental twaddle. Relationships between men and women meant, for him, a mutual attraction and having a good time together. He had never understood what Harriet meant when she started talking about the closeness of two people's minds. He'd known in the early days of their marriage that she wanted something more from him than he'd had to give and remembered saying to her: 'Look here, Harriet, I love you as much as I can love anyone. What more do you want?'

She seemed to accept that at the time, yet she'd gone on searching behind his back for what she thought she needed and now imagined Paul von Murren gave her. Well, he'd had enough, and it was high time Harriet learned that he, Tony, was her husband. He wasn't used to being pushed around by any woman, least of all by Harriet who had once so adored him. If trying to be kind and letting her have this holiday brought no reward, then he'd go and fetch her back.

Impulsively, Tony marched into Cooks and bought an air ticket to Innsbruck, following Paul's hurried journey of four days ago. As action suited his temperament, the mere fact of being on his way cheered him into a better frame of mind. He discovered an attractive Spanish girl sitting in the plane on the opposite side of the aisle and, before the first hour was up, had moved his seat into the empty one beside her.

The girl was beautiful in a typically Spanish way. She had velvety dark eyes, a large

244

sensuous red mouth, black straight hair knotted Grecian fashion high on the back of her head. She was chic to her finger-tips, wearing a smartly tailored English tweed dress beneath a very becoming mink coat. Her sheer nylon stockings revealed long, beautifully shaped legs. But Tony had been struck most of all by the look in her eyes. If his own had been questioning, hers had most certainly answered him and he had no fear of a rebuff when he moved over beside her.

'Cigarette?'

She smiled straight at him and drew off her suede gloves in order to take a cigarette from the silver case he held out to her. The gold bracelet on her arm jingled as she did so.

'It's nearly lunch time. I think we should have a drink before we eat. A cocktail? Sherry?'

When the air hostess had brought the drinks, Tony settled back comfortably to find out more about his travelling companion. He could never resist the challenge of a pretty woman, and she was certainly that. Moreover, she was exactly the type he understood, who played his game his way.

It seemed she was half Spanish, half American. She had been married and widowed and was now touring Europe.

'To try to recover from the sadness of losing my husband,' she told him, a look in the dark eyes far from any sign of the sorrow of which

245

she spoke. Tony was intrigued, as much by her broken English accent as by what she said. She was clearly very well off. She had been recently to Paris to buy a few clothes, she told him, mentioning some of the best fashion houses. Then to London, for only in London could one find a really well-tailored suit, and now to Innsbruck for a week for some sunshine and perhaps a little ski-ing before she returned to New York where she lived.

'My name is Dolores del Carlos,' she finally introduced herself. 'Now, pliss, you tell me about you?'

'I'm Tony Harley,' he said, holding her eyes with his own half-smiling glance. 'I, too, am on my way to Innsbruck. I had intended to go through to the Piller Lake where I have . . . er . . . friends. But I might stay a day or two at Innsbruck if the ski-ing is good.'

They both knew he had no intention of remaining for the ski-ing. Dolores del Carlos knew Tony's type just as well as Tony knew hers. They understood each other's language and Dolores only hesitated a moment before replying.

'That would be very nice. We would have the chance to further our acquaintance!'

'I hear it can be very lively in the evenings there,' Tony went on, grinning. 'Dancing—do you like dancing?'

'Ver-ry much. You will be staying at the Sporthotel?' She named one of the best hotels,

246

just out of Innsbruck.

'Of course,' Tony said quickly.

'I have been there before and it is comfortable and amusing,' Dolores said smoothly. 'Sleigh rides, *lugeing* and an ice rink.'

'Never a dull moment, in fact,' Tony laughed. 'It should be fun.'

It was fun . . . just the kind of fun Tony liked most.

They even went ski-ing together, hiring equipment for the day. But Dolores was at her best when she appeared dressed for the evening, undoubtedly the most attractive woman in the hotel, and Tony, handsome and debonair, made just the right foil and companion for her.

Dolores del Carlos was certainly no fool. She knew Tony was attracted to her and, after two days, even a little in love with her. So far as she was concerned, she was more than ready to fall in love with him. Five years of marriage to a very rich but middle-aged American businessman had given her all the luxuries she craved from life, but none of the physical stimulus her passionate nature craved. When he died suddenly, Dolores had been left very well off and she was determined to look around carefully before she married again. She had no intention of allowing some young American to marry her for her money. Tony was no American and clearly he, too, had money of his own. He had plenty of charm and plenty of experience with women. Dolores was not blind to the fact that he possessed all the right touches and used them deliberately whenever he thought it might gain his own ends.

As to those ends, Dolores did not have to be blind to guess what he did want from her. But she didn't mean him to have what he wanted . . . not yet. So long as she was toying with the idea of a second husband, she meant to remain uncommitted.

Within the space of two days in which they were constantly together, she made up her mind that Tony would suit her perfectly. She had discovered that he had a job which meant little to him in London and that he'd often thought he might enjoy life in America better. The only thing she had not discovered was that he already had a wife.

Tony deliberately withheld this fact from her. He had hoped on the plane coming over that his two days in Innsbruck with Dolores would be a casual and amusing little love affair. Dolores had led him to believe that she was in agreement with his ideas—her eyes, her repartee, her gestures all confirming his belief that she found him as attractive as he found her. But he had been more than a little piqued to find that while she had permitted him to kiss her passionately in the moonlight outside the hotel after hours of intimate dancing together, she had in fact locked her bedroom door when he knocked on it later.

He'd recovered from this temporary set-back by morning and was his usual carefree self when he met her for drinks in the lounge at midday. But when evening came again and once again he held her tantalizingly supple body unresisting against him as they danced, he said:

'Dolores, you aren't being fair. You promise everything and give nothing.'

She laughed her deep husky laugh and her dark brown eyes looked into his, mocking him.

'I promised nothing, Tony. Besides, my dear, we are almost strangers, and tomorrow you are going away.'

'Does that make a difference?' Tony asked, sulking. 'If I stayed . . .'

'But you will not be staying,' Dolores said. 'You have twice told me you have to go to Kitzbühel soon to see these friends.'

'I could come back this way,' Tony said meaningfully.

'But perhaps not,' Dolores said. 'And perhaps I, too, will be gone by then.'

'But dash it all, Dolores, I want you,' Tony said, pulling her back roughly into his arms. 'Don't you know how irresistible you are? It isn't fair to a fellow . . .'

'Come, Tony, you are behaving like the spoilt little boy who cannot get his way. As a matter of fact, I find you very attractive. And I am ready to admit that I want you, too. But I think not just for one night, Tony.'

Tony started to think. Dolores was right, they would want a deal more time than one night. In fact, they hit it off so well in every other way, that he could well imagine himself spending weeks in Dolores' company and still wanting more.

Yet there was Harriet to think of. He could of course stay on and not go to the von Murrens at all. They certainly did not expect him. On the other hand, he'd made up his mind to break this thing up between Harriet and Paul once and for all. No one was going to cheat him behind his back and make him look a fool.

But did he really want Harriet back? Wasn't he in fact happier without her? Suppose he really went ahead with his threat and divorced her? But he couldn't get a divorce, he knew that. Harriet had never given him grounds. All he could do was blacken von Murren's name. He could let Harriet divorce him. Then he would be free to have those weeks with Dolores if he wanted them.

Did he want them? She was a very attractive woman—far more sophisticated than Harriet; far more fiery and no doubt far more passionate. Yet Harriet had not lacked passion once, and despite his attempts to think otherwise, Tony knew that his wife had far more depth to her nature than he or Dolores del Carlos would ever have.

Tony wrestled with his feelings far into the night. What was it about Harriet that had always got to him just when he most wanted to escape? What was the power she had over him? Was it just that his vanity baulked at the idea of any woman falling out of love with him? Or was it more than that? Was it that deep down inside him he recognized Harriet's true worth as a wife and respected her? She'd been the only woman in his life he'd wanted to *marry*, yet in many ways the least suited to his needs. Dolores was far more his type than Harriet could ever be. Wouldn't he be far happier married to a woman like Dolores— perhaps Dolores herself? There would be much to be said for such a marriage. Dolores had money . . . and they could live in New York where he firmly believed there was never a dull moment. How bored he often was in London, with the same old faces, the same old round of night-clubs.

But Tony could not bring himself to let Harriet go. There was something about her . . . even now he could imagine the look in those incredibly green eyes of hers and feel himself tantalized, almost hypnotized by that intangible quality that was the essential part of her, and that had never quite been within his reach.

'You'll be here at least another two days, won't you, Dolores?' he said at length. 'That

251

isn't long to wait. I'll be back in two days and we'll talk about us again then.'

'I'll be lonely without you,' Dolores said, laughing at him, for he knew full well that there would be at least half a dozen men who would be ready to take his place the moment he left her side.

Once on his way to the *Schloss*, away from the physical proximity of her personality, a little of Dolores' hold over Tony vanished and he became once more the angry, resentful husband. Harriet's treatment of him became exaggerated in his mind as the train sped through the beautiful scenery, all of which Tony missed, for he had no eye for the beauties of nature except in so far as they were portrayed by the female species! His thoughts were all with his young wife and what she might be doing at this moment with Paul.

When Tony arrived, Paul and Harriet were out walking in the forest. The *Gräfin* had insisted that they spend at least an hour or two away from the sick-room, and since she was supposed to sleep after lunch, she had given them to understand she would be happier and more able to sleep when they were not there.

In fact, she did not sleep. She was aware with some strange insight that death was approaching, and she wanted desperately to see as much of her beloved son as time allowed her. She had really seen so little of him since the war had ended and he had left

252

home. A few weeks here and there . . . no more. She could have died peacefully, she told herself, if only she could know she was leaving Paul a happy man. But it was all too clear to her how deeply he was suffering. When he was unaware of her glance or Harriet's, he would look at the girl with such longing, such sadness, that her own heart felt near to breaking for him.

Yet there was nothing she could do . . . nothing. She would have gladly given her blessing to a divorce but Paul could not and *must not* give up his career, not even for Harriet whom she had grown to love like her own daughter.

It might have been easier if I had hated her, the sick woman thought unhappily. Then I could have made Paul see how he was wasting his life. But she's all he needs in a wife, gentle, loving, sincere, good, in fact everything I would have chosen for him myself. And she loves him, too . . .

Twisting and turning in the great bed, the *Gräfin* wrestled with her thoughts. She was startled to hear the door open, for she had told the nurse not to disturb her until Paul and Harriet came back. As she looked up, she saw a strange young man standing in the doorway.

'I say, I am sorry. I've come to the wrong room. The maid said the second on the right. I am so sorry.'

Tony was extremely embarrassed. He

253

guessed at once that he had come into the *Gräfin*'s room. He'd been going to wait in the sitting-room when Maria told him Paul and Harriet were out walking, and now he'd bungled in here, of all places.

'Come in, young man, and introduce yourself. Sit here beside me where I can see you.'

Tony moved awkwardly into the room. He hated sickness in any form and the thought that this woman was dying made him even less willing to do her bidding. But weak though her voice might be, even hard to understand, there was still sufficient command in it that he felt he must obey.

'I'm Tony Harley, Harriet's husband,' he said, when he was seated in the bedside chair. 'As a matter of fact she doesn't expect me. I suppose I ought not to barge in like this uninvited, but the truth is—'

'You've come to take your wife home,' the *Gräfin* finished for him.

Tony felt his resentment at Harriet fly to the surface, making him forget that he was an embarrassed intruder in the room of a dying woman—von Murren's mother at that.

'Well, after all, what else should I do? I dare say you know she's in love with . . . with your son. And he's in love with her. No husband is going to stand for this kind of thing.' His voice trailed away as he saw the blue eyes, one so twisted and visionless, the other so alive,

254

watching his lips.

'Yes, I see your point of view, Mr Harley. But you should not judge your wife unheard. There is nothing between my son and your wife of which either need be ashamed. I can assure you of that.'

'But how do you *know*?' Tony asked with petulance. 'Apparently they are out walking now. You don't know what goes on except when they're in here with you.'

'Mr Harley,' the voice was suddenly clear and sharp. 'You apparently do not trust your wife. I do! And I trust my son.'

Tony had the grace to look uncomfortable.

'Well, I grant you may know von Murren better than I do. All the same—'

'You have had cause to mistrust your wife in the past?'

'Well, not exactly,' Tony admitted. 'That's to say, she's never done anything that—well, never actually done anything wrong. All the same, she is in love with von Murren and I'm not taking any chances, that's all.'

The *Gräfin* was finding the conversation extremely tiring and had to muster all her strength not to show it. She was at last learning a little more about Harriet's husband. Harriet had never criticized him, never spoken of him disparagingly. Only Paul had told her the kind of man he was.

'Perhaps you tend to judge others by your own standards,' she said pointedly. 'You do

255

not trust anyone because you, yourself, are not to be trusted.'

Tony bit his lip, uncomfortably aware that her point had gone home.

'We're all human,' he said at last. 'I don't expect Harriet or von Murren to be different from anyone else.'

'Nevertheless, they are a little different,' the old woman said quietly. 'Surely you have found out, in these years in which you have been married to Harriet, that she is essentially good. I do not say she is above temptation. I do say, however, that she would never give way to it.'

'Well, what would you do if you were in my shoes?' Tony said at last. 'My position is hardly a pleasant one, knowing my wife is living here in the same house with the man she loves. Wouldn't you want her home?'

The *Gräfin* looked at Tony steadily.

'That depends, young man . . . depends how much you love her. I think if you really want her back, you should let her have her way now. She will be grateful to you for trusting her and she will be in your debt for putting your wishes second to hers. A woman, especially a woman like Harriet, will do a lot for someone to whom she feels she owes something. I think she would really do her best to settle down and make a go of your marriage. To drag her home now would be to make her resentful and unhappy and would gain you very little.

256

Besides, Mr Harley, I do not think you will have long to wait.'

Tony looked at the twisted, suffering face and for the first time in his life he felt suddenly ashamed. Here was a woman dying . . . or near to death, in great pain and half paralysed. He'd come, a stranger, into her room and had burdened her with his own problems. He didn't know what to say. The *Gräfin* spoke again, her voice tired now despite her determination not to show this angry young man how exhausting he was for her.

'You would be more than welcome to remain here, near your wife,' she said slowly and with difficulty, 'if this would solve your problem.'

It was on the tip of Tony's tongue to say that this was the very last thing he wanted. A grim old castle stuck halfway up a mountain, most of the interior encased in gloomy dust-sheets, and an old woman dying by minutes—hardly a very cheerful place to have a holiday! Besides, there was Dolores . . .

'I . . . I don't think Harriet would want me here,' he said, shifting the blame quickly. 'If you really think I'd do better to let her stay on, well, I don't want to make her unhappy. It's just that—well, I suppose I am a bit jealous. I'll have a chat to her when she comes in and then I'll push off. I'm sorry to have disturbed you. I hope you'll be better soon.'

'No, I think that is the last thing you would

want,' the old lady said with an attempt to smile. Tony had the grace to colour at the tactlessness of his remark, and the *Gräfin* softened.

'You know, young man, I should dislike you. But for you, my son could be a happy man. I have so often wished you did not exist. But now I have met you, I don't dislike you. I am just a little sorry for you . . . you are so young . . . so very young . . .

Her voice trailed off as a sudden spasm of pain caught at her heart, making her breathing difficult.

Tony looked round the room frantically for help. He saw the bell-rope and tugged it violently. Within moments, a nurse came into the room and, glancing at the bed, went quickly to the table and took some tablets which she gave to the *Gräfin*, speaking to Tony in a language he did not understand.

'English,' he said desperately. 'No speak Austrian.'

A faint smile crossed the girl's face and she said in broken English:

'You go now. Patient very tired. Come back later.'

Tony needed no second bidding and was soon closing the door of the sick-room thankfully behind him.

As he stood in the stone passage wondering quite what to do now, he heard voices . . . Harriet's voice, and presumably Paul's.

258

'. . . so beautiful here, Paul. The forest is like a fairytale wood.'

'More beautiful than Hampstead Heath? Or the Hog's Back?'

Harriet laughed.

'Far more lovely. I'll go and see Maria about some tea.'

Tony stepped forward, Harriet's happy laugh ringing tantalizingly in his ears. He hadn't heard her laugh like that for—for years!

'Tony!' The smile left her face as she saw him, whitened beneath the sun-tan, and then flooded with colour. 'Tony, I didn't know you were coming! How long have you been here? Why didn't you send me a telegram?'

Tony shrugged his shoulders and nodded at Paul, who stood silently at Harriet's side.

'I thought I'd surprise you, Harriet!' He gave a short laugh without humour in it. 'As a matter of fact, I'm not staying.'

'Perhaps you would care to talk to Harriet alone,' Paul said stiffly. 'Will you take him to the sitting-room, Harriet? It is warmer in there.'

'I don't think we've really much to say to each other,' Tony said bluntly. 'But perhaps a good chat wouldn't be a bad idea after all. I think you should be in on it, von Murren.'

'If you wish,' Paul said.

Harriet escaped for a moment to tell Maria to bring tea for three to the sitting-room, and then, reluctantly, she rejoined the two men.

259

They both rose to their feet as she came into the room, Paul first, for his manners were always impeccable. Tony also when he saw Paul get up. When Harriet was seated, Paul said:

'I hear from your husband that he went into my mother's room by mistake. It seems she had some kind of attack, so I'm going along to see how she is. I'll be back in a moment or two.'

Alone with Tony, Harriet sought for something to say. Tony was watching her face in a way that made her uncomfortable. It was almost as if they were strangers.

'Why *did* you come, Tony?' she asked the question again. 'To ask me to go back with you?'

'Frankly, yes!' Tony said, watching the colour rush to her cheeks again. She was looking miles better, he thought. The sun-tan suited her and she seemed to have put on a little weight. As always, Harriet still attracted him. He needed to be away from her from time to time to see her anew, to feel the old excitement that had first made him want to marry her. It was a pity their marriage had gone wrong after such a promising start. She'd been frantically in love with him at the beginning. When had she changed? Had it been his fault? Admittedly he'd cooled off a bit, and there'd been that affair she'd found out about. But she'd got over it and they'd

260

been pretty well all right until the baby came.

He frowned, feeling, as he always did when he recalled that accident, guilty and uncomfortable. In many ways he'd been pretty hard hit himself by that business. He'd been proud to be a father and it gave a fellow a strange feeling of satisfaction to see a human being he'd helped create. It hadn't been entirely his fault he'd been drinking that night. That crying had got on his nerves. He'd been damnably sorry afterwards, but Harriet wouldn't have anything to do with him; wouldn't even let him talk about it. Unfair, really. Still, she had got him out of a lot of unpleasant publicity by the way she gave evidence at the inquest. At least she was loyal enough then . . .

Of course, von Murren was really to blame. He'd stepped in and caught her on the rebound. The old flame turning up at the psychological moment just when Harriet had stopped loving him. And now what?

'*Would* you come back if I asked you?' he enquired, seeing all too clearly the distress cloud her face.

'Yes. I'd come,' Harriet said helplessly.

'Mind you, I've not made up my mind yet,' Tony said, not intentionally sadistic, but needing somewhere inside himself to hurt her as she hurt him by her indifference to him, by her way of making him seem in the wrong without actually saying anything. 'I think that

261

old woman knew what she was talking about when she said I'd stand a better chance of making you love me again if I give in now.'

'You discussed me . . . with Paul's mother?' Harriet asked, horrified. 'Oh, Tony, no!'

'Well, it was her idea!' Tony said defensively.

Harriet drew in her breath.

'You shouldn't have worried her . . . not now, when she's so ill, Tony. Our affairs aren't important enough.'

'Perhaps not to you,' Tony said quickly, 'but they are to me. Frankly, Harriet, I don't see any solution. You admit to my face you love someone else—hardly a very pleasing thought for me, your husband.'

'Tony, please! I'll come back with you now. Don't let's talk about it any more.'

'I've come here for the express purpose of talking about it,' Tony said, his temper rising. 'I've honestly come to consider these last few days that I'm being a bit of a fool. I've humbled myself to ask you to forgive me. I've given in to you whenever I could. And what do I get out of it, I'd like to know? A wife in love with her doctor!'

'Tony, Paul isn't my doctor any more. Please, *please* don't let's talk any more. I'm sorry I asked you to let me stay. I'll come home now . . . today. I'll go up and pack.'

'Perhaps I don't want you back!'

He hadn't meant to say it but the desire to

262

provoke her had taken the upper hand.

'Not . . . not want me?' Harriet barely whispered the words.

'Well, why should I? I'd like a wife who puts me first for a change.'

'Tony, that isn't fair. For years I did just that.'

'And I suppose it was my fault you stopped. You'll go on blaming me all your life because of that wretched accident.'

Harriet's face was white and tense.

'That isn't true, Tony. I don't blame you any more. It might have happened to anyone.'

'Oh, yes, I know! But *you* know I'd had a few too many that night. And you'll never forget it. I don't think I want to spend the rest of my life under a cloud. I'm fed up with it all. I've a damn good mind to go ahead and divorce you.'

'You can't, you *can't*!' Harriet cried. 'There's no evidence, Tony. I've never been unfaithful to you.'

'The loving wife pleads with her husband not to leave him . . . I don't think!' Tony said with all the sarcasm he could muster, a sarcasm born of the jealous pride that was uppermost now. 'The loving mistress who doesn't want her lover's name besmirched.'

'That's enough! . . .' It was Paul's voice, like a whiplash across the room. 'I dare say I ought to stay out of the picture and let you get on with your attack on your wife. But I'm not

263

going to. I've stood by long enough. Go ahead and do your worst. Cite me as co-respondent if you choose. Do you think I wouldn't live down all your accusations? Do you think I couldn't raise any evidence against *you*? Do you think a divorce court would accept your word above mine when they have a list of all your many love affairs? Two can play your game, and I have a fair idea who'll come off worse.'

'Paul, don't . . . please don't! I can't stand any more. It's horrible . . .' Harriet said, remembering the old lady perhaps dying in the room next door.

'I've stood by long enough,' Paul said, his face taut and his blue eyes ablaze with anger. 'How can he stand there throwing insults at you? I believed I had no right to come between husband and wife. But what kind of a husband has he proved to be, Harriet? He's been unfaithful to you more times than he can probably name.'

'You can't prove that!' Tony was standing now, facing Paul with a confidence he was far from feeling.

'I could. I can prove you tried to make love to Eileen. I could no doubt bribe that housekeeper of yours to tell me a few things which have happened in London when Harriet wasn't there . . . affairs you were silly enough to brag to Eileen about.'

He turned to Harriet who was now standing too, white as a ghost.

264

'I'm sorry to disillusion you, Harriet, but I think it's time we all spoke the truth. While I believed you still loved him, I couldn't say anything. Well, go on and deny it, Harley. Now's your chance to clear your name . . . if you can.'

'Tony, it isn't true, is it?' Harriet asked. Though she might not love him, he *was* her husband, the man she had married and lived with all these years. She couldn't bear to think that he'd been deceiving her all the while.

'Still the trusting little innocent!' Tony sneered, having no defence, so resorting to attack and then to bragging. 'Maybe it is true. Von Murren can't prove it, but if you really want to know, he's right. Other women find me attractive even if my wife doesn't.'

'Oh, no!' Paul broke in. 'You're not going to make Harriet feel it's her fault you went to the bad. It started years ago . . . didn't it?'

He was guessing now but he thought he knew Tony's type well enough to be sure he could never be faithful to any woman for long.

'If you've been looking for evidence on which Harriet could divorce me, you've been wasting your time,' Tony blustered. 'Harriet condoned those offences so they won't hold water.'

'Then you admit there were . . . others?' Harriet whispered, collapsing into the nearest chair and covering her face with her hands. 'Oh, Tony, *why*?'

Tony had the grace to feel a first glimmer of shame. After all, Harriet had loved him very deeply once and even then he'd not been able to stay faithful to her. Suddenly honest, he shrugged his shoulders and said:

'I suppose it just isn't in me to stick to any one woman,' he admitted, so casually that Paul felt his anger boil to the surface again so that he wanted to strike out and hit this man with a physical force that would show his contempt for him.

'You married the wrong woman,' he said through clenched teeth. 'I dare say there are plenty of the type to suit you. Yet you had to have Harriet . . . the most loyal, trusting woman you could ever find.'

'Paul, don't . . . this is doing no good . . .' Harriet's voice trailed away miserably.

Tony went over to the window and lit a cigarette.

'So where do we go from here? You two love each other. I suppose you're both hoping I'll step out of the picture and leave you to your wonderful noble love. Why should I?'

'Harriet won't come back to you now,' Paul said, trying to keep the violence of his feelings under control. 'You've nothing to lose now, Harley. Cite me as co-respondent if you wish. Blacken my name if you choose. I'll take that risk. But be warned that I'll blacken yours if I have to use a whole force of private detectives to do so.'

266

Harriet was on her feet now, standing between the two men, her hand laid restrainingly on Paul's arm. If he were to antagonize Tony now, Tony might go ahead, just to get his revenge. Nothing must come between Paul and his career . . . *nothing.* She turned her face to Tony beseechingly.

'Please, Tony, don't listen to him. He doesn't mean it. I will come back . . . I promised I would. You mustn't take any notice of what Paul says, *please* . . .'

Tony looked down at her, despite himself filled with a strange respect and admiration for this woman he had married.

'You really do love him, don't you, Harriet? Even to the point of living with me again if it'll save his skin. Well, you did the same thing for me once, at the inquest. I admit I was drunk that night . . . that I was fully responsible for the baby's death. No, don't deny it, you know it's true. But I paid the price in another way . . . it was the end of our marriage, wasn't it? You could never have loved me again after that. It's odd really, but I began to want your love then as I'd never done before. I suppose I'm just that type who always wants what he can't have.'

Harriet's green eyes were widened in surprise. Only once before had she heard Tony speak with such humility, such honesty about himself. He wasn't really bad—only weak.

'This is the end, I can see that,' Tony went

267

on. 'There isn't much point trying to make a go of our marriage now. So I'll give you your freedom, Harriet . . . and take mine. For heaven's sake don't look so desperate. I'm not going to attack your precious Paul. I'll give you evidence and you can divorce me. When it's all over you can marry him and good luck to you.'

Harriet's face was a mirror of her changing emotions. Fear was replaced by doubt, surprise and finally hope.

'Tony, do you really mean that? Is that what you want yourself?'

Perhaps it is, Tony thought. Perhaps I'll be happier with a girl like Dolores. I won't have to feel guilty with her . . . as I suppose I've really always felt with Harriet. Harriet's too good for me. I can't live up to her ideals. I never could.

'Yes, that's what I want for myself,' he admitted.

He heard the door close and, turning his head, saw that Paul had left the room. He grinned with a return of his old humour.

'Tactful sort of chap, your future husband,' he said, but broke off as he saw the tears running down Harriet's face. He put out a hand instinctively but let it drop again to his side. 'Dash it all, old girl, what's there to cry about?' he asked, embarrassed as he always was by the sight of a woman in tears.

Harriet blew her nose like a small girl and attempted a smile.

'It's just that I can't quite take it all in, yet,' she said in a choked voice.

'I thought this might make you the happiest woman in the world,' Tony said gruffly.

'Yes, but you . . .' Harriet faltered. 'What will *you* do, Tony?'

He couldn't tell her about Dolores but he knew he would be taking the next train to Innsbruck to rejoin her there. He felt a lifting of his spirits at the thought.

'I'll be all right,' he said with conviction. 'I expect I'll take a bit of a holiday now I'm out here. There's no need to have me on your conscience, my dear. Surely you know me well enough by now to believe that I never act unselfishly.'

'I don't think I really know you at all, Tony,' Harriet said truthfully. 'You seem to be so many different people, and I'm not sure even now which is the real you.'

'Perhaps I'm not sure myself . . . and I want to find out,' Tony said with rare insight. 'Come on now, Harriet, cheer up and come and see me off. I suppose I might walk down to the village and get a taxi. Like to come along?'

The half-hour walk through the pine forest was, to Harriet, one of the happiest interludes she had ever had with Tony. He seemed to have a new gentleness about him, a new understanding. They discussed what they would do with Henry VIII and the mews cottage, agreeing that each should keep one to

269

live in until they chose to sell.

'I might go to America,' Tony said, thinking again of Dolores. 'Always thought I'd like a trip out there. Who knows but I may even decide to stay out there. As for you, you'll be marrying Paul, so you can get rid of the cottage then. Meanwhile, there's the question of money.'

'No, Tony, I don't need any money. You've always been so generous I've enough saved in my account to keep me for months.'

As they approached the village, Tony stopped and put his hands on her shoulders.

'No need to come any further, Harriet. We can say our good-byes here. You know, you've been a pretty good wife and I think Paul's lucky to be getting you. I'm sorry it all had to turn out this way . . . but I suppose it is all for the best. I've never been much of a husband to you.'

'I'm sorry, too!' Harriet said, still unable to believe that this really was the break-up of her marriage . . . perhaps the last time she would see Tony.

Tony grinned ruefully. 'You know, when I set off from London I'd every intention of taking you home with me. I'd certainly no intention of telling you you could divorce me. Funny how things work out. It just came to me suddenly that we'd never be happy together after all that's happened. You really believe you'll be happy again with von Murren?'

270

Harriet nodded her head, unable to trust her voice.

'Well, I'll be pushing off. So long, Harriet, and . . . try not to think of me too badly.'

He bent and kissed her lightly on the cheek, taking one last look at the girl he had married and knowing that she had become a stranger to him. His mind was already leaping ahead to the future . . . to the bright lights and the music of the Sporthotel at Innsbruck and to the fascinating woman he believed would be eagerly awaiting his return.

Harriet slowly retraced her steps up the hilly path.

It was all over . . . finished. Tony was going to let her divorce him and one day soon she would be free to marry Paul . . . *Paul*.

Her thoughts swung violently to the man she loved . . . her first love. Her heart began to beat faster as she realized at last that she was free to go to him . . . free to love him as she had once before so many years ago. She knew that now, after all this time, her love was of a different quality. She had been a girl then, young, inexperienced, innocent, immature. Now she had so much more to offer him . . . Paul . . .

As if in answer to her silent cry, she saw him coming towards her through the trees. She ran towards him, seeing his arms open to receive her, his face alight with tenderness and a love to equal her own.

'Oh, darling, *darling*!' he whispered, holding her so close against him that the beating of their two hearts seemed to merge into one. 'I still can't believe it's true. Tell me he really did mean it, that you are going to be free to come to me—to marry me! Harriet, tell me you love me . . . say it.'

'I love you, Paul, more than anything in the whole world.'

His lips were on hers, gently at first and then with increasing strength as his feelings, always so rigidly controlled, at last broke free. He covered her face with his kisses, her eyes, her forehead, and again her mouth. She clung to him, afraid of the mounting desire that she felt in answer to his and yet glorying in it too. She belonged to him body and soul, heart and mind. She was Paul's love. Her need of him was equal to his need of her. Soon—not soon enough—they could be married, man and wife, and she could be truly his.

Again sensitive to her thoughts, Paul broke away with a trembling sigh.

'I must not kiss you like that again, Harriet. I dare not answer for myself, and you don't belong to me yet. I want to wait, my darling— to wait till you are my wife.'

She touched his lips tenderly with her finger-tip. He caught her hand and pressed one last kiss on the palm. Then he linked her arm through his and smiled at her.

'Come, dearest, we'll go home now. We

must tell my mother. She'll be so happy for us.'

They walked close together, their sides touching, their hands entwined.

'I wonder if her talk with Tony wrought this change in him,' Harriet said thoughtfully. 'I wonder what she said to him . . . what made him so different?'

Paul wondered, too. What an odd fellow Harley was. One moment cruel and threatening, the next a reasonable, even likeable enough chap, offering his wife the divorce she wanted. Somehow he could not bring himself to believe that Tony was activated purely by gratitude. It was true Harriet might have saved him from a charge of manslaughter. But that had been months ago. Something had happened since to make him change his mind. Another woman?

He kept his thoughts from Harriet. It could do no good further to disillusion her about the man she had married. He ought never to have revealed what he knew about him, but he had had to protect her from Tony and make her see how dangerous he was. He knew Harriet would have gone back to her husband despite her knowledge of his past affairs, openly admitted by him, in order to save him, Paul. And he could not have permitted her to make such a sacrifice for him. Perhaps Tony had seen for himself that threats to blacken his name were useless now that he knew Harriet loved him. But it didn't matter any more—the

273

reasons were unimportant beside the outcome of that strange half-hour. Harriet would be free at last, and he could ask her to marry him.

'I'm so happy . . . so unbelievably happy,' Paul said. 'If only this good news can help to make my mother better!'

But it was a vain hope, and one that even Paul did not really believe in. The *Gräfin* died in the early hours of the following day. Her last hours were happy ones. When Paul and Harriet had come in together, hand in hand, to tell her the news, she realized that there was no further need for her to fight against death. Her son was happy . . . his future a bright star of happiness that she could see already in his eyes. And Harriet, the girl who had become so dear to her, happiness shone from her eyes too, as they looked at Paul, filled with the kind of love she knew would last their lifetime.

They told her of their plans for the future and, tired though she was, she encouraged them to go on talking long into the night. It made her so very content, to see the joy and happiness that radiated from them. When at last they left her, she lay back against her pillows, the pain in her heart gathering momentum, but the glow of happiness remaining, warming her, comforting her, up to the end.

'She must have been in great pain!' the young nurse said, distressed that her patient had not rung for her when the last attack came; that she had not been there to offer what help and relief there was. 'Yet her face is so happy, so peaceful. I have not seen her look so wonderfully content since I came.'

'Yes, she does look happy . . . and very beautiful,' Harriet said, holding tight to Paul's hand as they stood side by side in the presence of death. She knew how terribly shocked Paul had been when the nurse woke him to tell him the dreadful news. She, too, had been deeply shocked and very distressed, for Paul's mother had come to be far dearer to her than her own mother.

Lucy Carruthers was married to Bernard now, and living in the South of France. She seldom wrote to her daughter with whom she had so little in common, and they had all but lost touch.

Paul's grief was a deep, silent one, and though he stood quietly now beside the bed, Harriet could feel the terrible sense of loss that must be his.

The nurse tactfully left the room and Harriet was about to go too, but Paul reached for her hand and said:

'No, don't leave me, Harriet. Stay with me.'

She remained beside him, helping him by her mere presence to get the better of his grief. When at last they left together, he could even smile, saying:

'I know my mother so well, Harriet. While she knew I was unhappy she wanted to go on living despite the pain, hoping there might be something she could do for me. Last night she knew I had everything in the world I wanted. I believe she gave up fighting, knowing her job was done . . . that you were there to take over. It's because of you, Harriet, that the end was at last welcome to her. I think she wanted to go. I shall always be grateful to Harley for coming when he did.'

Harriet could understand. Her own maternal instincts could appreciate so well a mother's love for her son. And Paul's mother had spent a whole lifetime striving for his good and his happiness.

'I'll make him happy . . . take care of him . . . love him,' she whispered her silent farewell.

*   *   *

It was 1956. So much had happened since Harriet and Paul were last at the *Schloss* together. They had left it that May morning a week after Paul's mother had died. Now they were returning, hand in hand, walking through the woods towards their first real home together, and it was again May. The air was warm with sunshine, the gentians, a brilliant blue amongst the other wild flowers, opening their petals to the call of spring. Everywhere they turned their heads to see, there were signs of new life. On the mountain slopes below the forest, the calves and baby goats jumped about

276

in the deep grass at their mothers' sides. And Harriet felt the same promise of life stir within her.

It was three months now since she and Paul had married quietly in England. They had not hoped it could be so soon but fate had brought an abrupt end to the divorce proceedings. Tony, true to his word, had gone to America. Although he was not yet married to her, he had been living with Dolores in New York and they were on their way to the Bahamas for a holiday when the plane crashed, a disaster which took the lives of all the passengers and crew.

Harriet, who had been living alone at the cottage while Paul continued his course in London, had read of it in the daily newspaper only an hour before a telephone call from Tony's solicitor had advised her of the facts. She had been very shocked, having no thought to the effect on her own life, but only a horror at the unnecessary death of anyone so young and full of life as Tony had been. But the solicitor had made her understand the difference this would make to her. The divorce would never be heard now . . . she was a widow, and free to remarry whenever she chose. Harriet had not wanted her freedom at such a cost. She bore Tony no ill-will. It did not occur to the solicitor that she could still be fond of Tony—sufficiently so to be deeply upset by the news of his death. He was surprised when he advised her of Tony's will the following day, to see tears in her eyes. Tony had left everything to her.

'Oh, but I can't take his money,' Harriet had protested. 'You see, I haven't really been his wife for months and—'

'He made this will after you had started divorce proceedings against him,' the solicitor broke in. 'The fact is, I advised him to put his affairs in order before he went out to America. He'd never made a will and I thought he should do so. He said he couldn't be bothered and that he was quite happy for everything to come to you in the event of his predeceasing you. I pointed out that you wouldn't be his next of kin once you had obtained your divorce, so he told me to draw up a few lines, making it clear that the money was to come to you in any event. I remember his very words. He said: "She's a sensible girl. She won't waste it, and she deserves it more than anyone else I know."'

Talking it over with Paul, Harriet had seen a way out of her predicament. She did not want the money for herself, but she did not wish to refuse it out of deference for Tony's generosity of spirit. So it was decided that the entire sum, amounting to £80,000, would go to Paul's clinic.

Money had come pouring in from other sources. Harriet's brief encounter with the American girl on the train to Austria had borne surprising results. Gifts had come, too, after the *Gräfin*'s death, although she herself had left only a little beside the plans for the transformation of the *Schloss*. Friends like the Hauffmans had sent cheques and work had already begun when Tony's legacy was put at their disposal.

Now it was nearing completion and Harriet alone knew the tremendous feeling of gratification this had given Paul. Not only had his dreams for a tubercular clinic been realized, but there was sufficient money to staff it and run it for years.

It seemed to Paul, as he walked beside his wife, his arm around her shoulders, that his cup of happiness was full. The double tragedies of his mother's death, and then Tony's, had made so much happiness possible for hundreds. No one knew better than Paul what this clinic would mean to the suffering, to the children and to the parents who until now had had to watch their children die slowly through lack of space for them in the hospitals and sanatoriums. His mother had understood his vision of the future, and so had Harriet. But it was Tony's money which had paid the final bills and wherever he might be he must surely be glad that no matter how useless his life had been, his death was going to mean so much to so very many.

And he had Harriet here at his side . . . Harriet who meant more to him than anything

279

in the world. He would not have believed it possible but now he knew that with each day he loved her more; that marriage had brought them closer in spirit as well as in body. They were now so much part of one another and now she was going to bear him a child.

He felt sure that it would be a boy, the son she had once longed for, the son they would call Paul, who would be the living symbol of their love for one another. In the grounds of the *Schloss*, the 'lodge' that stood at the castle entrance had been converted into a comfortable and simple home for them. Here he would be near the wards where he would do most of his work. Here his son would grow up, where he himself had spent so much of his childhood, in the fresh clean air of the Austrian mountains, where nature was clean and pure and like champagne. Here he and Harriet would live and work and grow old together . . .

He stopped for a moment, leaning his face against her hair, feeling its softness against his cheek. Then she turned her face and gently touched his lips with her own.

'Come, darling,' she said, smiling. 'We're so nearly home.'

Hand in hand they went onwards and upwards until they disappeared from sight through the trees.